About the Author

Anne Scott was born in London and studied at the Aida Foster Theatrical School before moving to the south coast when she married.

She appeared in many films and television shows as well as working as a model.

She opened the Anne Scott Agency in Bond Street, London in 1977 and went on to produce some of the best Central Feature Fashion Shows at major exhibitions and was the innovator of choreographed fashion shows.

Sex Drugs Rock and Roll

Anne Scott

Sex Drugs Rock and Roll

Olympia Publishers
London

www.olympiapublishers.com
OLYMPIA PAPERBACK EDITION

A CIP catalogue record for this title is
available from the British Library.

ISBN: 978-1-78830-874-8

Although the novel is fiction it is based on some real events, such as
the 40th birthday party for Christina Onassis and the 21st for the
then Lord Althorp Spencer. The book is based on my experiences
as a Model Agent

First Published in 2021

Olympia Publishers
Tallis House
2 Tallis Street
London
EC4Y 0AB

Printed in Great Britain

Dedication

This book is dedicated to my wonderful family

Acknowledgements

There are a few special people that I would like to thank in helping me with this novel.

The first is my darling daughter, Lulu, who helped me remember our time running the model agency, we had a lot of fun putting the stories together

My thanks also to, Richard Sotnick, who gave me invaluable advice with the publishing contract.

When times were tough some of my darling friends helped in more practical ways, Erika Crocker, Grazyna Dallas, Jaci Davison and Hedley Greentree.

My Thanks and Love to you all

Chapter One
1960

'Where was the new store that everyone was talking about' thought Annabel. She had walked for what seemed like miles up and down Kensington and still couldn't find Kensington Church Street. Annabel had saved her money from her last modelling job, which was crap, both the job and the pay, but she needed a new dress and she had heard that a shop called Biba was the new best thing. At last she saw a sign 'Kensington Church Street' and there was the store. It looked very unexciting but as she had spent so much time already, she would just go in.

She pushed open the door expecting to hear lots of noise, girls milling about and music playing but there was just silence. It was so strange inside, lots of people with dresses over their arms, and it was so dark. Black walls, lots of clothes which looked all the same, and a few coat-stands with feather boas flung over them. And then she spotted THE DRESS. It was priced at £4.10 and she had just about enough money. It was just what she needed to wear for the party this evening. She needed to look both glamorous and grown up, not just a middle-class girl who was only seventeen but a successful model who knew how to mix with the powerful people who had steady jobs and their own flats.

She had met Michael and his friends in the coffee shop

close to her agency in Bond Street yesterday, and they had asked her to join them. It might have been because her photo was in the Daily Mail that day and they thought that she was a top model.

"Come and join us love," said Michael after he had spotted her alone at a table. The crowd he was with looked exciting. There were four boys who all looked like they had regular work and spent their money on the most fashionable clothes of the day, but it was the girls who interested Annabel the most. They looked so much older than her, with the latest beehive hairdos and their makeup was just amazing. Black heavy eyeliner, false eyelashes and white lips. She could just see her mother letting her go out looking like that — some chance.

Her mother was great, paying for her to attend a school that got jobs in showbusiness when they were old enough. Annabel knew that she wasn't talented like some of the girls at the school, but she was pretty and had a good figure, so modelling had seemed to be the best option when she left school. But her mother just did not understand that she needed to be in with the right crowd, not sitting at home in East Finchley waiting for the phone to ring.

Michael had told her that he worked at a bank and his friends worked in the city but didn't explain exactly what they did. The party that night was at Michael's flat and she did not want her mother to have a heart attack when she saw her in her short new dress and latest hair and makeup. She needed a plan.

"Hi Zofia, its Annabel, I need to ask you a really big favour." Zofia was Annabel's best friend from school, and although she hadn't seen her in a while as Zofia was working on a TV series, lucky bitch, she knew that in an emergency she would help. "I met a really nice boy yesterday and he has invited me to a party tonight, but I need somewhere to change as Mum will not let me go out late."

"No problem" said Zofia, "but you will have to let yourself in, I will leave the key under the mat, and tell your mum you are staying with me tonight in case you are really late." Zofia was lucky as she lived in a flat with two other girls who were also in the TV series and she didn't have to answer to anyone. Zofia only had her mum as her father had died when she was a baby and the two girls had grown up together, not like her father who had walked out on her mother and her when she was just nine years old, and they had never heard from him again. Next, she needed to phone home and tell her mother that she was staying with Zofia and then watch out world, Annabel would be ready to party.

Annabel felt very nervous as she stood in front of the door, just about to knock when the door opened, and a strange young man stood there.

"Are you a friend of Michael? You can come in if you have bought some supplies."

"Sorry," said Annabel, "I didn't know you had to bring a bottle." With that, the young man who wore a very strange outfit of really tight trousers and a brightly coloured shirt with a waistcoat covered in beads and sequins started to laugh. "No, my little friend I mean something to smoke," with that he left Annabel at the door and just walked away.

Annabel shut the front door and entered the room where the party was in full swing. The air was heavy with sweet smelling smoke, and the music was very loud with a Beatles record playing. All the guests were drinking, and it seemed that everyone was smoking. The room was like a scene from a play with brightly coloured clothes in satin, silk and many other fabrics, all with beads and baubles. It even seemed that some of the men were wearing makeup!

Annabel just stood there not knowing what to do. Should she try and find Michael as he had invited her and could introduce her to some of his friends? Just then one of the girls she had met with Michael at the coffee shop appeared in front of her. "Hello little girl, why aren't you drinking?" She reached out and took a glass from a table with what looked like wine in it, "Here you are, drink up, that will make you in the party mood."

Annabel took a gulp of the drink in her hand and started coughing, it tasted foul and was very strong but after a few minutes it didn't taste so bad and made Annabel feel very lightheaded. Within a few minutes Annabel was in the middle of a crowd of people, all of them talking and smiling at her, and then someone grabbed her hand and started to dance with her. She didn't know who he was, and it didn't seem to matter, the noise and heavy atmosphere was making her feel good.

Someone handed her a strange looking rolled-up cigarette and told her to inhale slowly. Which she did. The room was starting to spin, and Annabel was feeling very good indeed, her head felt very heavy and she seemed to be nodding like a dog. A mellow feeling came over her, it felt like she was on a cloud. Her eyes were half open, and she thought someone was holding her hand and leading her away from the party to a quiet place where there was only the sound of muted music. She suddenly felt herself on a soft cushion and a lot of hands were trying to take off her clothes, which was OK as she felt very hot.

Hands were gently stroking her legs and she felt her

knickers come off, Annabel wished that she had bought some new underwear as her bra and pants were old and a dirty grey colour from so much washing. She then felt a cool breeze over her whole body and a soft voice was saying how lovely she was. Hands were then on her breasts and fingers in her, lips were sucking at her nipples which felt so good when suddenly she felt a weight on her body as if something heavy was laying on top of her and something hard was pushing into her, and she heard a noise like someone grunting. It sounded like Michael's voice and she didn't like this at all, if this was love why didn't it feel good. Then the whole room exploded in a bright light and everything went black.

Annabel opened her eyes very slowly and tried to look round the room she was in, which seemed to be a very large bedroom with the frilliest furniture she had ever seen, all in pink. Everything was pink, the walls, the chairs and the bed linen. It must be a woman's bedroom she thought, but it was not like her bedroom at home and she did not know where she was. Then it all came back to her, the party, the drink, the funny cigarette and then she remembered being brought in here and someone had raped her.

She sat up and looked round for her clothes which she saw on the floor by the bed in a heap. Her lovely new dress was torn and did not look fit to wear, but she had to get out of this place and forget everything that had happened to her. She must phone Zofia and ask her if her mother had phoned to ask where she was. She hoped that Zofia had told Mum that she was asleep. She was sore and very angry and when she next saw Michael, she would ask him what had happened to her.

Annabel thought that she should put this unhappy experience behind her and just try and move on. When she was rich and famous, she would show him. She got out of bed, dressed and left by the front door. The house was a mess with people asleep everywhere, but she just wanted to get out and forget she had ever been here.

The door slammed behind her as she walked into the street and hailed a cab.

Chapter Two
1975

She was bored, so bored. The children were out with the au pair and David, her husband, was away again at sea. She had met David through some friends during the summer of 1961 and he just swept her off her feet. Older than she was by some ten years and so handsome. He was an officer in the navy, stationed in Portsmouth and within just six months he had proposed, and they got married and he had bought a lovely house on the hill overlooking Portsmouth Harbour.

She now had four children, Barry the oldest, twins Gemma and Poppy and her baby, Simon. David looked after her so well, gave her everything she desired but he was away for most of the year and she missed him. When he was at home they went out, parties with the other officers, dances on board, holidays on the Med; it was such fun, but he was hardly here and what was she supposed to do? Just sit at home knitting!

Annabel thought that she would go shopping to Commercial Road as she had heard that there was a new boutique just opened and wanted to check it out.

The shop front looked fun, all crazy clothes in the windows and music blaring out. She pushed open the front door and entered an Aladdin's cave. Brightly coloured clothes hung from the rails, all in the latest fashion; hats, scarves and bags adorned the walls, just hung on giant hooks. This looked like fun. She could spend a few hours trying on outfits and she could afford to buy something from the allowance David gave her each month.

From the back of the shop came a smart lady who Annabel recognised from one of the parties David had taken her to.

"Hi, you're Annabel, do you remember me? I'm Charmaine, but everybody calls me Charlie." Annabel smiled at Charlie, she thought she looked nice. "Please just look around and when you've finished come and find me and if you have time perhaps, we could go out for a coffee"

Annabel spent the next hour trying on everything in the shop and found a great mini skirt and top, very Mary Quant, that really suited her. When she took it to the till to pay, Charlie was standing by the till serving another customer.

"Let me have that," she said and took the outfit and put it into one of the shop's bags. "You can have that one me, if you can help me with an idea I have. Let's go for a coffee and I can tell you all about it."

Charlie led Annabel outside, and they found a coffee bar close by. When they had ordered and were comfortable, Charlie explained what she had in mind. "My boutique is really new and although I have many customers, I need more people to know about us, so I thought that I could put on a fashion show and invite everyone I know together with their friends. Although I have the clothes and can style the show, I don't know how to go about putting a fashion show together. I heard that you were a model in London so thought I would ask if you could help me"

Wow, thought Annabel, I can't believe she has just asked me to do this. "I would love to help and I know lots of girls who could model, and we could dance instead of just walking up and down. I was trained as a dancer so it would be easy for me, but we would need lots of rehearsals so the girls knew the moves. Where could we rehearse? And we need really upbeat music."

"Hey, don't worry about that. My husband has a large room at the back of his shop we could use, and I know someone who could provide a sound system. You just think about the scenes and I will style it"

Annabel and Charlie spent the next hour working out everything and Charlie promised she would be in touch as soon as she found a suitable venue to hold the show in.

Annabel drove home with her head in the clouds, lots of ideas floating round. She could start a model agency and provide models for all the local shops, and what about photographic jobs, and she would organise shows that would be dance fashion shows not just the boring shows that people went to see now, but exciting fun shows, wait until she told David about this, she hoped he would be supportive and not throw a dampener on the idea.

The next weeks just flew by, there was so much to organise, and she met with Charlie every day so that they could exchange their ideas and discuss which ones would work out best. Charlie had booked a room in the Guildhall in Portsmouth for eight weeks' time, so Annabel needed to book her models and organise the rehearsals.

Annabel spent the next three days just sitting on the phone and speaking to the prettiest girls she knew, if they could dance that would be a bonus. One of her friends, Lindy, was a dancer at a local club and said that she would help her. Everyone she spoke to said yes, they would love to be part of this fashion Show, and within a week Annabel had booked sixteen models and had also spoken to Dave who would organise the music for the show. Everything was ready to go, music selected, scenes thought through each with a theme, so Charlie could style it, fittings and rehearsals were also booked. Charlie had also organised some people backstage who would help with dressing the models. Annabel thought that she would also appear in a couple of the scenes as she loved dancing and it would help if the girls could see what she wanted and could copy her.

The day of the show came around and Annabel was so excited but also nervous. What if it all went wrong? The girls might forget their moves. Dave could put on the wrong piece of music. Some of the clothes that Charlie had organised might not look so good. There were a thousand things that could go wrong, and it would be all her fault.

The lights in the room dimmed and the first piece of music started which was the cue for the first scene to begin. The next hour went by so quickly; music, lights, clothes thrown everywhere backstage as the girls hurried to change into their next outfit, suddenly it seemed it was over, and the models went on stage to take a 'curtain call' followed by Charlie and Annabel to take a bow to thunderous applause.

Annabel had taken off the last outfit and went out front to see some of her friends when a lady came up to her with a big smile. "I thought that the show was fabulous, I didn't know there was another model agency in Portsmouth, what's it called" Annabel thought quickly "Annie's" she said, and so the Annie's Model Agency began.

Chapter Three
Four Years Later

Annabel had done well in the last few years, but she now needed to spread her wings. The best work was in London so an office was what she should open.

Her first big job had come from a London client who had phoned the local TV station and had asked for a recommendation. Someone at the station had heard that she did fun dancing fashion shows and had given Joe her phone number. The show was on a ship that was docked in Portsmouth Harbour and Annabel had met with Joe who was a lovely, sweet, gay man who really wanted to be on the stage himself, not just the PR man for the London Fashion company he represented. The show was organised using the best models she had on her books and Lindy helped with the choreography. It was a great success. Joe promised her that he would recommend her to some friends in the fashion business but told her she really needed to be in London to make the agency a real success.

So here she was in the Kings Road with an appointment to see a promotion company that had offices. She was shown into the office that was on the second floor and was large and airy with some desks in the middle where sat some great looking girls who were busy on the telephone. It all looked very exciting and had a real buzz about it. This is what I want thought Annabel, a London base in the middle of where everything was happening.

Annabel was shown into the office of the owner of the agency who was a very smart and elegant lady called Sophia Reed.

Sophia made Annabel feel at ease immediately and was interested in the work she had done, asking lots of questions about the proposal Annabel had told her about. Annabel explained that she produced dance fashion shows and already had many interested clients who wanted to talk to her about forthcoming shows they wanted to put on.

"I know that you specialise in promotions and I only do fashion shows," said Annabel, "so we would not be in competition but could probably help one another, all I need is an address in London and a desk so that I can call clients and make appointments to see them. I also can use any of your own girls who were not working." Sophia thought that this would be a great idea as she wanted to expand the promotions and by helping one another this could work really well. She also had space in her office to let Annabel have a desk. They spent the next few hours together expanding on the ideas and promised to meet the next week as Annabel had an appointment to visit the exhibition organiser who was putting on the first Motor Fair in London and wanted a fashion show as the central feature.

The visit to the organiser of the Motor Fair went well and Annabel promised to let him have a quotation for providing the show; models, dancers, sound, chorographer, stylist and the latest fashion. Annabel spend a lot of time thinking about what she could do and putting together a really good price as she knew that as her first big event it had to be not only

fabulous and exciting but at a price that the Motor Fai
buy into.

At her next visit to meet with Sophia, she showed her the proposal together with the quote she had put together. "I thought that I would ask the organiser to build a slope on the stage that looked like a road so that the dancers could come down it at the beginning of each scene and also we could reveal the car of the show at the end of the show at the top of the ramp."

"Sounds good," said Sophia "I'm sure that you will win the contract, your ideas are really original."

They then spent more time talking about how they would go about organising the shared office space, and Sophia said that as soon as Annabel had installed a telephone her girls could take messages and then pass them on to her when she was not in London. All this sounded good, but first Annabel needed the first contract so that she had enough money to contribute towards rent and rates.

A week went by and Annabel still had not heard from the Motor Fair office, so she called them but was put through to a secretary who promised to pass on her message. Another week went by and still no contact, so Annabel telephoned again and this time she was put through to the managing director who sounded a little strange, not as friendly as he had been at her previous meetings.

"So sorry Annabel but we have decided to go with another company, the other company has a good track record, has been in the business a long time and their ideas and price was better than yours." Annabel took a deep breath before she asked the question, but she had a bad feeling that she already knew the answer. "Can I ask who the company is?"

"The Show Company, perhaps you know the owner Sophia Reed."

Annabel put the phone down very slowly and took a deep breath, she wouldn't cry. She would get even and the first thing she needed to do was to get an office of her own, no shared office space this time. Somewhere where both models and clients were happy to visit, and it must be central London.

Annabel phoned every estate agent listed in the phone directory and over the following few weeks visited every office that she felt sure she could afford. The best office she could find was in the Kings Road, no matter that it was the same location as that bitch Sophia, all was fair in love and war.

The office was on two floors with two small rooms on each floor, the first rooms consisted of a room big enough for a sofa bed and armchair and a bathroom alongside, above was the floor she would use as the office, the first room on this floor was where she would have a secretary to answer the phone and display the photos, the second room which was just slightly bigger was going to be her office and looked out onto the Kings Road. There was a cupboard on the landing where she put in a shelf, so she could have a kettle and make drinks. The washing up could be done in the bathroom downstairs. On the first floor was a dentist and he seemed a nice man and was happy to see many good-looking girls go up and down the stairs, so all was good.

Now she needed to contact as many clients as she could, make appointments and interview models and dancers to put on her books. Where to begin?

Chapter Four
1980

Annabel telephoned all the friends she had made through her modelling work and from school and told them about the new office in London and asked if they might be interested in registering. She had so many positive replies and arranged for the girls to come in and show her their portfolios as she knew that to represent them, she needed all the information as well as good recent photos. She had heard that models needed 'Z-cards' with both photos and measurements as well as the name of the agency printed before she could get work in. She also arranged for a company to come in to quote for the cards, so another good piece of work done!

Over the next few weeks Annabel interviewed the people she had called as well as friends who were in the business who wanted a new agency. Both girls as well as a few boys called in and she had, within a very short time, a good selection of both models and dancers.

Next on her agenda was to start contacting prospective clients as she wanted to make a name for herself as the leading agency for Dance Fashion Shows.

First on her list were all the exhibitions organisers. She phoned everyone listed in the Exhibition Bulletin that she could and made appointments to visit so she could explain in detail what she could offer.

Her first appointment was with the London Boat Show at Earls Court.

Annabel was very nervous when she arrived at the office in Earls Court which was tucked away at the back of the building. She had invested in a large portfolio where she displayed the models and dancers on her books as well as photos from the show she had produced on the ship in Portsmouth.

The organiser she met was very nice and helpful and told her that they would be interested in a central feature fashion show and would provide the stage, lighting and dressing room but the show had to be self-funding in terms of the production.

Annabel left the meeting with a renewed sense of determination.

She could do this and would make it successful. This was just the first step and now the hard work must begin.

Annabel had booked a very nice girl to help her in the office, Marion whose father was a doctor.

Marion worked just three days a week answering the telephones and making appointments for models to come in and show their portfolios. This worked as Annabel could then make appointments to meet up with clients when Marion was in the office. Annabel's mum also came into the office when things got hectic and this seemed to be working well. Her mother seemed to enjoy her time in the office, and was not criticizing Annabel like she used to. She also was helpful in keeping the office tidy, answering the telephones and organising the shelves with the model photos.

During the last few months Annabel had made good contacts and there was also quite a lot of work coming in for promotional staff and showroom modelling. Joe from the show on the ship had passed her name onto other clothing manufacturers as well as booking models for his company, so Annabel was making enough money to pay the rent and the other expenses but she still had to break into the big time.

She had received a call from a television company in Southampton who had passed her name onto a film director who needed extras for the film he was shooting on the south coast. This was fun and Annabel telephoned all her friends in Portsmouth to see if they wanted to earn some money for filming over a couple of days. The people booked did not need an Equity card as this was just extra work. Although it was quite low paid it sounded like a fun thing to do and everyone who Annabel called said, "Yes please." She organised at least 20 extras as well as six children. She sorted out the contracts and booking forms for each person. Not a lot of commission but it all helped and was something more she could add to the list of credits the agency was involved in.

She next telephoned all the leading stores in London to see if they were interested in sponsoring a fashion show as the major feature at the London Boat Show. One of the stores who had shown interest arranged for Annabel to come in and meet the managing director the following week.

The next few days were very busy as she had to present a quotation for the show. She telephoned Lindy from Portsmouth who had worked as a choreographer on her first dance show and asked if she could meet up so that they could discuss whether she could help with the show. She also spoke to Charlie as she needed a stylist. Both the girls were interested, and Annabel arranged to meet up with them when she was home.

The girls all met up in the same coffee bar Charlie and she

had used before, so they could discuss what they needed. "First, we must get some dancers and models who you can audition in London, but we should wait until after my meeting with the managing director. I will arrange a studio to hire, I have heard that Pineapple Studios are good and not too expensive, and Lindy you can come and stay with me as I have a small flat. I will also put an advert in the Stage newspaper saying I am looking for some new dancers and models." Lindy and Charlie were both excited as this was a new venture for them.

They worked out how much to charge for the production and Marion in the office could type it up. Annabel had headed paper with the Annie's Agency printed on it so all she needed now was to make a good impression at the meeting.

The morning of the meeting arrived, and Annabel carefully selected her clothes. She did not feel a mini shirt was the right look so she chose a smart tailored suit with a shirt with a big floppy bow at the neck and the highest shoes she felt comfortable in.

She arrived at the corporate offices and announced herself to the receptionist who asked her to wait. Annabel had brought with her a portfolio showing photos of the models and dancers she represented and a selection of photos from the shows she had produced both in Portsmouth and on the ship.

It felt like forever sitting and waiting but when Annabel looked at her watch only five minutes had gone by. When she looked up a very smart lady was walking towards her smiling. "Hello, you are here to see Robert Chase. Please come with me."

Annabel was shown into a large office overlooking Oxford Street, the carpet was thick, and she felt like she was walking on cotton wool. The managing director Robert Chase stood up to greet her. This was the first time that Annabel had been in this position where she had to sell the benefits of a large-scale production. She knew that what she was offering was a new and exciting format that had not been done before as fashion shows were rather staid affairs with models just walking up and down a catwalk showing off the latest fashions. In fact, when she was working before she married, she had been booked as a catwalk model in the very store that she was visiting, but this was something she was not going to talk about. She wanted to impress this man as a businesswoman.

"This is an exciting opportunity for your stores to be a major feature at The Boat Show. It has never been done before as the only clothes being shown at the exhibition were sailing gear not high street fashion, and every lady who goes sailing likes to change into something glamorous at the end of the day."

Robert Chase came from behind the desk and sat with Annabel so he could look through the portfolio. He asked her about the work she had done, what was involved in producing a show, how long the preparation would take and how many times a day the show would be seen.

"We need to work with the fashion buyers to understand what you want to show then we will set the look into scenes. The whole show should not be longer than twenty minutes as we want the audience to stay and not move away. The show will be on the central feature stage three or four times a day for the length of the Boat Show Exhibition which is ten days."

Annabel handed over the quotation which she had produced bound into a smart folder.

"Thank you, Annabel, this all sounds, very interesting and I want to discuss this with the other directors before we make a decision, so I will contact you in a few days to let you know our thoughts."

Annabel stood up collected her portfolio, shook hands and left.

When she got into Oxford Street, she was shaking but rushed to get a taxi to return to her office.

Annabel rushed up the stairs, she was so excited she wanted to telephone Charlie and Lindy to let them know how she had got on.

When she entered the office one of the male dancers Austin was pacing the floor and looked in a terrible rage.

"What's the matter Austin? Just calm down and come into my office so you can tell me what the problem is."

"I have just had the most serious unpleasant experience of my life and it is all the fault of Marion. As you know I was going away for a few days and needed a new passport. When I was telling Marion that I needed to get the photo for the passport signed by a doctor or other professional, she told me not to worry as her father was a doctor and would sign the photo for me. I was standing at customs at the airport and was stopped and told that the signature on the back of the passport was fraudulent."

Annabel went into the office where Marion was sitting and repeated what Austin had just told her. "It's not my fault I was just trying to help, my dad said he could not sign the photo as he did not know Austin, so I signed it myself." With that, Marion flung the papers she was holding on the desk. "I am not working here anymore. This place is rubbish and I am leaving now!"

With that Marion collected her coat from the rack and stormed out of the office.

Austin and Marion looked at each other in amazement, oh my God what a situation. Austin could see that Annabel was upset with both the passport issue and now she had no one to help as a booker in the office.

"Don't worry Annabel, I have a friend who lives in London and is looking for a job as a booker, I will telephone him immediately to see if he is still looking and arrange for him to come in to see you."

Austin telephoned and his friend Freddie who said he would come in that afternoon to meet Annabel and was available to work.

The day had been both exciting and horrific but hopefully she would get the contract for the Boat Show and Freddie would be her new booker.

Freddie came in to meet Annabel and was a lovely gay guy. He was very enthusiastic about the job and although he had not had much experience working as a booker, he had a great personality and appeared to be organised, and most importantly he could type and did not mind what hours he was needed to work.

Annabel booked him to start working the next day and told him that she would spend as much time as was needed to show him the ropes and explain the workings of a booker.

Austin had calmed down and had left the office with a promise of photographic work that week and a list of auditions that he could go to. 'Go sees'" were an important part of finding work and sometimes the models had to attend several in one day, sometimes meeting the same models and dancers at the castings. One of the castings the next day was for a commercial and if Austin was booked, he could be paid for the day of shooting as well as royalties each time the commercial was shown.

The telephone was ringing constantly over the next week with bookings, but Annabel was still waiting for the call about the Boat Show and felt that as she had not heard from Robert Chase perhaps, he was not as interested as it had appeared.

She thought that starting tomorrow morning she would phone some more potential sponsors but as it was getting late, she would close the office and head home. Just as she was turning off the lights the telephone rang,

"Annie's Agency, can I help you?"

"This is Robert Chase's PA. He would like to meet up with you in the next few days to discuss the Boat Show in London. Can we arrange a time?"

Annabel ran down the stairs with the biggest smile on her face that could have lit up the whole of the Kings Road, she couldn't wait to get home and phone Lindy and Charlie with the news.

It was now September and the Boat Show Exhibition opened in London early in the New Year so lots of hard work lay ahead. She was going to make her first dancing fashion show the very best that anyone had ever seen; a first at The Boat Show and the first in London.

Chapter Five
1981

The next month flew by with organising the major feature at the Boat Show. She had secured the contracts from both the organiser and the stores and they were now sitting proudly on her desk.

Lindy and Charlie had come up to London to see her new offices and to work out a format for the show content. Annabel had arranged for both the girls to meet with the fashion buyers so the clothes they would be showing could be incorporated into scenes and music would then be arranged to compliment them. Lindy and Annabel had arranged to visit Dave the sound engineer in Portsmouth where he had a studio so that they could listen to the music and lay down tracks onto a cassette for Lindy to use at rehearsals. Next an audition had to be booked at Pineapple Studios and an advert placed in the Stage newspaper so dancers could attend.

The day of the audition arrived, and the girls arrived at the studio and were amazed to see a crowd of people lined up outside. "What's happening?" asked Annabel to the receptionist after they had pushed their way through the crowd "The dancers are here for your audition as there is not much work in January unless you are in a West End show."

There were so many talented dancers it was hard to choose, but at the end of the day they had a list of 10 who were booked for the exhibition and at least 20 more who wanted to be represented by the agency. Some of the dancers that auditioned were rude when they were told not to wait but would be contacted by the agency, but that was to be expected as it was hard to be told 'No thanks.' Annabel made a note of who had an attitude so that she could put them on a list NOT to see them again.

As they left the studio and walked into Covent Garden to get a taxi Annabel spotted someone at a bus stop that she thought she recognised. When she looked again, she knew who the man was, Michael from the party she had gone to all those years ago when she had been raped. What on earth was he doing standing at a bus stop, he had told her that he worked in the city and although he had not said exactly what work he did she had assumed he was a highflyer.

"Girls would you mind if I didn't come back with you, as I have something really important I need to do." The girls went off by taxi to Waterloo station to get a train home after arranging a time to all meet up the following day.

Annabel walked towards the bus stop, she knew she was looking good with the latest look, hair and makeup perfect. Michael watched her crossing the road. There was no recognition in his eyes, so Annabel was not going to enlighten him that they had met before.

Michael stepped in front of her smiling, "Hey little girl what are you doing for the rest of my life."

"Waiting to catch a bus home," she said smiling sweetly. "Want to grab a coffee?"

They walked to the nearest coffee bar, sat down and ordered some drinks.

Michael told her that he worked in the city, and he was only at the bus stop to meet a friend to catch a lift as his Aston

Martin was in the garage. Same old chat-up line, same old story about his work. He was very good-looking and wore a nice suit, but when Annabel looked closely, she could see that the clothes he wore were only cheap knockoffs, and not the real McCoy. He obviously did not have a great job in the city but worked as a low paid worker or he would have the money to take a cab.

Annabel told him that she was a dancer but out of work now and was working at a department store just to make enough money for her rent. She told him that her name was Susan, and when he asked her to meet up, she readily agreed, but said she would call him to confirm a date. They left the coffee bar together after exchanging phone numbers.

Annabel was smiling to herself, time to get even, but first she had much more important things to do and a show to organise.

The next day she went to the sound engineer's studio to listen to a music selection and agree with the Lindy what would be used.

Dave's studio was a real mess with records piled high everywhere and sound equipment on several tables. Dave made Lindy and Annabel some drinks and told them they could smoke if they wanted.

Hours went by with record after record being played. The room was even a worse mess than when she had arrived with cups of cold half-empty cups and ashtrays overflowing with cigarette butts. Later that afternoon they had all agreed a good selection of currant pop songs which included, 'I feel like dancing' by Leo Sayer, 'Don't go breaking my heart' by Elton John and Kiki Dee, 'Daddy Cool' by Dark and 'Dancing Queen' by Abba. Dave said that he would organise the performing rights licence which they would need to play the music and he would have ready for Lindy a couple of cassettes for the rehearsals in the next few days.

Annabel needed to get home and spend some time with the children as David was still away. She had a really nice au pair from Germany looking after the kids and friends who were taking Gemma and Poppy to school each day. The boys Barry and Simon were weekly boarders at a private school on the Isle of Wight and did not need collecting till the weekend.

She drove home slowly her head filled with the music she had heard that day. As she entered the house all was quiet. She knew the twins were with friends having tea but where was Elke the au pair. She called out a few times but no answer. When she went upstairs Elke's door to her room was closed but she could hear noises from inside. "Elke I am home, can I come in."

"I will be out in a few minutes, see you downstairs."

Very Strange, Annabel waited in the kitchen until five minutes later a very subdued Elke came in. "I am sorry but I had a friend visit me," with that a man Annabel had never seen before come into the kitchen, he was putting on his jacket and looked like it had been a very long time since he had had a wash. "Sorry mate I am just leaving" with that he opened the front door and slammed it shut behind him.

"Elke, who is that man? You know I have never stop you from having friends round here. This is your home while you live with us, but I don't think you were just having coffee. I do not like to think you are inviting strange men into my home that I do not know, you are here to look after the children, and all I ask is that you respect this." Elke burst into tears and ran upstairs to her room.

Annabel waited as she needed for Elke to calm down before she spoke to her as she liked the girl and the children loved her, she also did not want to have to look for a new au pair as so much was going on with the agency now and she needed help at home as David was away for the next few months.

After about an hour Elke came downstairs, Annabel could see she had been crying and felt sorry for her, but the children must come first and if Elke was to stay a few rules needed to be set out.

"I was so lonely as I haven't seen my boyfriend in many months and Richard was kind to me and has taken me out for a few meals so I invited him home just for a drink. I am sorry but things got out of hand and then you came home"

Annabel went over to give Elke a hug. "Elke if you like someone and want to have a relationship that is up to you but please not here in my home. I need to trust you and if we are to go forward this must never happen again."

They sat and spoke for the next hour and Elke told her that she wanted to make some more friends as she felt that all she was doing was looking after the kids or going to college and studying. Annabel promised Elke that she would phone some friends of hers that also had au pairs and try and arrange for them all to meet so that Elke could have some more friends and a better and enjoyable time while she was in England.

The twins arrived home and were delighted to see Mummy and wanted to tell her all they had been doing at school and ask for permission to go on an outing with some friends the next weekend. After the children had eaten, had a bath and been put to bed by a now much happier Elke she sat down for a much-needed rest.

Having four children at home as well as an au pair was like having five children to look after, models were so much easier — or so she thought.

Chapter Six
Payback Time

Annabel booked a studio for the rehearsals, organised for Charlie to select the clothes and arranged fittings for the models and dancers. She had met up with Robert Chase to give him an update on progress and the store manager where they were getting the outfits, so all was in hand. She needed some commentary to use between scenes, just a short explanation on what was being shown and where the clothes were available. Lindy had reported that rehearsals were going well, and Annabel told her she would call in just to say hello and see what had been set.

Christmas came and went in a blink of an eye. Unfortunately, David was still away at sea so could not join them. Annabel was getting really fed up not seeing her husband but the other officers' wives were in the same position so she couldn't complain to them, but she missed having him at home. No conversation, no meals out, no fun and no sex. Perhaps she could do something about that, she was meeting so many people and going out for a meal or whatever was just what she needed.

Having time to spend with the kids was fun although she had to tell Gemma off many times as she was rebellious and no matter what she was told to do she had an answer. Poppy, her twin, was quiet and had a sunny nature and was happy to go along with anything. The boys were just content to be at home as they did not like to be away during the week at school, but both were doing well and had many friends. Barry was leaving school in the summer and did not yet know what he wanted to do. "Can we come and see your show before we go back to school. We're old enough to walk round on our own." She promised that she would take all the children up to London before they went back to school and make it a nice day out.

Annabel had heard from Michael as he had phoned many times, so was very keen. He asked when they could meet, and they arranged a date. It was just before the Boat Show and as David was still away, so she would not need to offer any explanation on why she was staying overnight.

Annabel had thought very carefully how she would get even and had arranged a really nice surprise for Michael and bought some things that would help her with her plan.

She arranged to meet him at his flat. She knew where Michael lived but asked for his address as if she had never been there before.

She dressed very carefully with some brand-new underwear which she would throw away after that evening.

Walking up to the front door of Michael's flat brought back some unhappy memories of when she was last there, but now was the time for payback and he deserved all he was going to get.

The front door opened after Annabel had rung the bell. "Hi Susan come in, I thought that we would just have a few drinks before we went out for dinner." Annabel followed him in to the flat which had been set up for a romantic evening. Low lights, music on the record player and a bottle of wine opened on the coffee table.

Annabel took off her coat and threw it on the chair. She was wearing a very short skirt and low top which left nothing to the imagination, just peeping up from the neckline was her lacy bra which from the interest in Michael's eyes was doing the trick.

The music was playing softly in the background and had it been another man or another place Annabel could have got in the mood. She sipped her drink slowly as she did not want to get tipsy, Michael had no such thoughts and drunk his wine quickly and poured himself another glass and bought out another bottle, most of which he drunk.

Serval hours went by and Michael was getting very drunk, he had moved close by then to Annabel and started to kiss her face, neck and his hands had moved under her top so he could caress her breasts. It felt nice. He then slowly began to take off her clothes, first the top and then her skirt and tights until she was just wearing her new underwear.

"Wow, you really are gorgeous."

"Michael, I really want to please you but let us take things a little slower. Can we move into your bedroom and let me give you a massage first and then let me do things to you that I think you will like?"

They moved into the bedroom with Michael hardly able to contain himself, kissing Annabel with every step.

"Just lay on the bed and let me undress you."

Michael jumped onto the bed and lay back with a big smile on his face.

First Annabel took off his tie, undid his shirt very slowly kissing him in each place that she exposed. Next, she undid the belt of his trousers and took off his shoes and socks. She pulled off the trousers and flung them on the floor. She ran her hands very lightly across his chest taking his nipples in her mouth and sucking while she ran her tongue round them. She moved slowly down his chest until she came to his underpants which she rolled down to expose his ridged penis. Rolling her tongue down the length of him she cupped her hand round his balls, playing with them. She then put a finger in her mouth and sucked it slowly until it was wet and then she put her finger into his anus which she could see excited him.

"Oh God Susan please let me fuck you."

"Not just yet. This is worth waiting for, roll onto your front so I can massage your back"

She moved her hands across his back kneading hard on his neck and working his muscles until she could feel him relax. She moved her hands down his back slowly massaging all the places she knew would excite.

"Now turn over."

She pulled his underpants off and threw them on the floor with his other clothes. Now he was laying on the bed completely naked with his penis throbbing and engorged. She moved her mouth close to him just blowing small light breaths until she was only an inch away and then slowly brought her mouth on top of him and closed her lips so she had him in her mouth, and moved her tongue round his penis until he was panting and begging for more. She slowly sucked him moving her mouth on and off while she continued to cup his balls and play with them.

"I want to give you an experience you have never had before Michael, and it would please me as well if I can tie you up, just loosely. I wouldn't hurt you but it will enhance everything we do."

From her bag she took out some thin rope which was strong and tied his wrists up and tied the rope onto the bedposts. She repeated this with his other arm and then tied his legs to the posts at the bottom of the bed. Michael just lay there happy to go along with whatever this fabulous girl wanted. He was ready, so ready.

Annabel moved over his body making sure that he could not move at all and that the ropes would stay in place no matter how much he tried to move.

"Now for the best part," with that Annabel leant forward so she could kiss his mouth, using her tongue. Then Annabel took from her bag a scarf and wound it round his mouth, she did not want to hear any complaints. Michael still looked like he was in for a good time and even when Annabel took a permanent marker from her bag, he was not aware that anything was not going to go the way he wanted. With the marker she wrote Rapist across his chest. Michael now was aware that all was not how it should be, and a look of fear came into his eyes.

He was wriggling around trying to move but the ropes held fast.

"This is payback time, to remind you to be nice to little girls, but don't worry, sometime tomorrow when I am not too busy, I will phone the police and tell them I heard noises from your flat. I am sure they will come in to investigate." She then pushed the marker into his arse.

Grunts like an animal in distress came from the bed and a wild look came into Michael's eyes. She could see that he wanted to be untied and set free, but Annabel just got off the bed and dressed slowly. She picked up her bag and at the door she turned and with a sweet smile she waved her fingers, shut the door quietly behind her and walked out.

Whoever had said the revenge was a dish best served cold knew just how that felt. Fabulous.

Chapter Seven
The Boat Show

Annabel arrived at the exhibition early to make sure all was in place. She had booked a nice wardrobe lady to look after the merchandise called Brenda who also was a seamstress so could mend any mishaps that occurred. Brenda and her team were there already sorting out the clothes onto rails for each model, clearly labelled into each scene with the model's name, with shoes and accessories beneath.

The dressing room behind the stage was not large so had to be organised. There was a row of mirrors attached to one wall and a long dressing table so that the models could do their makeup and hair. A long mirror was placed near to the entrance to the stage so the models could give themselves a quick look to make sure all was in place before they went on.

Next to the dressing room looking out onto the stage was a small room where Dave, the sound engineer sat. All his equipment was set up, but Dave was nowhere to be seen. Perhaps he had gone off to get a coffee.

The models were starting to arrive with their makeup cases and coffees in hand. Time to start the dress rehearsal as soon as Lindy and Charlie arrived, as they were driving up from Portsmouth that morning. Lindy was staying over that evening with Annabel at her flat.

Annabel was getting anxious, when Dave, Lindy and

Charlie arrived, and set to work immediately.

They spent the morning rehearsing without the merchandise just to make sure that the whole of the central feature stage was being used.

Annabel called a break so that the cast could have lunch. The afternoon rehearsal was not good as the models missed cues and the outfits did not look put together correctly.

The final dress rehearsal was better, but not yet quite perfect but Annabel felt that doing another run would not achieve much as she could see that they were all tired. The next morning was press day, starting at 11 a.m. so she called a rehearsal for 9 a.m. just to be sure.

They cleared up the dressing room so it would be ready early the next morning, collected all their personal belongings and left the exhibition.

When Lindy and Annabel arrived back at the flat, all Annabel wanted was a coffee and a bath, but Lindy was changing her clothes and putting on fresh makeup.

"Hey where are you going?"

"Hope you don't mind but some friends who live in London have invited me to a party, I promise I won't be back late," Lindy replied.

Annabel did not know how Lindy had the energy as all she wanted to do was collapse into bed. She gave her a key to let herself back in and said she would make up the spare bed for her.

As Annabel got into bed with so many thoughts running round her head and the music from the show playing on a loop. She felt her eyes closing and within minutes she was fast asleep.

The sun was shining through the windows as Annabel

woke up about 6 a.m. as she had forgotten to close the curtains. She looked over to the bed where Lindy was sleeping, and it was empty!

Where was Lindy? Perhaps she had decided to stay over with her friends and would arrive soon. Annabel got up, tidied up the flat, made a drink. It was now 7 a.m. and still no Lindy and no phone call. She would give it another hour before she had to leave, perhaps Lindy would make her way straight to the show.

Arriving at the exhibition at the same time as Dave and Charlie. She asked them if they had heard from Lindy, but they had no idea where she was. The main concern was perhaps she had had an accident. Dave was carrying one of the new mobile phones, a large contraption like a small suitcase, and heavy. Annabel always used a telephone box and carried a purse with coins to use for calls. She hated to be out of touch.

Dave promised to phone a few friends that both Lindy and he knew and see if he could find out where she was.

Rehearsals had to go ahead as the press were arriving at 11am and they had to be ready to perform a show.

With much trepidation Annabel called all the models together and gave them a 10-minute warning to get ready for the dress rehearsal. The show was good, so she gave them a break before the first show for the press.

Immediately after the press show she was asked to arrange for some of the models to dress so photographs could be taken on some of the boats. A hectic morning, what with photographers, a meeting with Robert Chase to make sure that he was happy with the show and worrying about Lindy who still had not arrived and there were no messages from her either.

By 4pm that day they were finished, the dressing room was tidy, and Annabel decided to go back to the office and check with Freddie to see if he had heard anything and to catch up with any messages and return any calls.

Arriving back at the office Freddie told her that he had made a few calls but no luck with tracking Lindy down. He gave Annabel her list of messages and bookings for some of the models that had come in.

Annabel went into her own office and scanned down the messages there was only one that was of interest from the TV company in Southampton, they wanted to speak to her about the possibility of Annabel auditioning for a new daytime programme. The format was a group of local businesswomen meet to discuss what was happening in their lives both with business and families.

She called through to the TV station and was put through to the producer of the show, Andy Peters.

"Hi Annabel, thank you for calling me back, I was wondering if we could meet up as I am at the moment putting together a list of guests who can appear in the new programme that's going out this spring."

"I would love to meet with you but I am at the moment involved in producing the central feature at the London Boat Show and would not be able to meet with you for the next two weeks but perhaps you might like to come up to London, see the show and perhaps then we can grab a drink."

"That sounds like a great idea. I always go to the Boat Show so I could look around and then catch your show."

Annabel arranged to leave a ticket in his name at the box office for two days' time.

Annabel was excited to hear more about the show and

thought that appearing on the show, if she got the contract, would help with the agency. She knew that she could not actively promote the name of the agency, but she could tell new clients what she was doing.

But she now had a more important and urgent thing to do, track down Lindy. It was getting late and she was feeling both worried and cross as this show was a big thing for her and if Lindy had just decided to do something else that day, she would have to have words with her, as having been let down so badly was not good.

Annabel went downstairs to the flat and decided to give it two more hours and then she would call the police.

At 9 p.m. the door opened, and Lindy walked in. There was silence for a few minutes before Lindy sat down.

"What happened? Where were you? I was so worried."

"I so sorry Annabel, but I went as I told you to a party with a boy I knew from back home, we had a few drinks and then someone brought out a cake they had made at home, I was starving so I ate a large slice, what I didn't know that the cake had been baked with some acid which caused hallucinations. I even thought that the walls were breathing. It lasted the whole night. I felt so weird as if all the furniture was moving and distorting in a dream-like way. I spent the rest of the night throwing up in the bathroom and then I just collapsed and slept the day away. I felt so ill, I still don't feel right, but I thought that I should just come here and explain rather than telephone you."

Annabel just looked at Lindy with amazement, what a horrible experience and she looked so ill, but in the future, she would have to make Lindy promise that when she was working, no more parties, no more going out late without leaving a contact number in case of emergencies.

She ran a bath for Lindy and made her a cup of sweet tea with a few biscuits as she did not think offering her anything to eat was a good idea as she didn't want her throwing up. After the bath she helped her into bed and turned out the lights.

Wow, what a day, worrying about her friend, running the rehearsals by herself, dealing with the press and a new contact for a TV programme.

Tomorrow things could only get easier and there was a lot to think about as Annabel shut her eyes and fell into a deep sleep.

Chapter Eight
Work

The first day of the exhibition went well and Annabel had the opportunity between shows of walking round the exhibition and speaking to some of the stands. She had made a few new contacts and asked them to watch the show when they had the time. She left her card and said if they had any questions to please contact her at the agency.

Over the course of the exhibition Annabel spent as much time as she could dividing her time between the office and meeting protentional clients on site. This was such a good opportunity to show the work that the agency did. She found time during the day to meet with Robert Chase to discuss the same deal for the following year. The organiser was happy with the central feature show as it had generated a lot of extra publicity for the exhibition and was happy to give the contract to Annabel for the following year on the same basis that it would be self-funding for the production.

The producer of the daytime TV programme had come to meet with Annabel and watched the show from the VIP lounge over the stage. He asked many questions as to how she had started the agency and what work she was involved in. They spent a pleasant hour chatting and when it was time for him to leave as he had not mentioned the TV programme Annabel just had to ask what the next step was.

"I hope you do not mind me asking about the programme and if you feel I am suitable and if I can audition."

"Sorry, I should have said, we would love for you to be a part of the show, perhaps when the exhibition has finished you could come down to the studios just to go through the contract and work out which shooting days you could be free for."

The following month after the Boat Show was very busy with many enquiries about shows and asking for models to come in with their portfolios for photographic and showroom modelling. She made appointments to discuss shows she could produce, and she had some good photos from the Boat Show to add to her list.

Freddie was working out well and seemed to be happy to be so busy. The only upsetting rumour she had heard through the grapevine was that some of the male models were being asked by Freddie to undress to their underpants so he could see their bodies. Annabel did not know if this was true, but she made a mental note to ask him about the rumour as she did not want to get known for anything like that. It seemed quite funny that the male models would undress but perhaps they just wanted a date with Freddie and wanted to show off how good they looked in the buff.

One evening when she was working late, Annabel heard some noises from downstairs and went to investigate. On the floor below she knew that an office had become vacant and wondered if a new tenant was moving in.

She was greeted by some men carrying large boxes into the room and a very petite lady was kneeling on the floor unpacking the most fabulous clothes she had ever seen

"Hi, I am Annabel, I have the two floors above you, and I run a model agency, can I help?"

"Oh, thank you so much, there is much to do, if I'm to be ready to show the clothes by tomorrow morning. I am an agent for a French designer, and I've already got appointments in the morning for customers to look through the garments so they can order for the next season. I must introduce myself I am Susie and I am very pleased to meet you. Any help you can give me I will be eternally grateful for."

What a nice dizzy lady Susie was, but Annabel was happy to help, just to look and touch the clothes was all the reward she needed.

They spent the rest of the evening unpacking and hanging the outfits on the rails which were already up. The clothes were just fabulous.

Bright colours for the next season, power suits with padded shoulders, coats in the most delicious fabrics, and the most glamorous evening wear Annabel had ever seen in silks and satin with heavy beads on the shoulders. Susie had sent out for something to eat from a nearby restaurant and Annabel had made coffees during the evening.

At last all was done, and both the girls were ready to leave.

"Annabel at the end of the season I sell all the sample outfits and you look like the right size; would you be interested?"

"Would I just, just please let me know when I can come in and please don't let anyone come before me. I would buy the complete collection if I could afford it but perhaps some key pieces would be great. Thank you, Susie."

Annabel was happy she now could extend her wardrobe with some good designer pieces at a fraction of the cost, and it would be nice to have an agent showing clothes in the building. It seemed a long time ago when she was counting the pennies to be able to have a new outfit, and now she was buying the clothes herself not just relying on David to give her an allowance. Best of all in two weeks' time David was coming home for some shore leave. She really missed him and was excited to bring him up to date with all her news.

Chapter Nine
Family

David had arrived the night before and the children just wanted to be with him, they spent some days out at the weekends as a family. David had bought a small boat which he kept at Gosport Marina and they spent some great times visiting the Isle of Wight for day trips. Annabel always brought food to the boat for them all but there always seemed to be extra people to feed. David collected people on his way to the boat or at the Marina, who wanted a day out on the boat. She was getting cross as these new 'best friends' just wanted to be looked after and never seemed to help either with clearing away lunch or washing the boat at the end of the day.

"Thanks David, great day out just let us know when you are going out again." Some chance thought Annabel.

One of the men brought his girlfriend with him and she spent the whole day at the front of the boat sunbathing in the smallest bikini Annabel had ever seen. After lunch she just put her finished plate on the deck without any effort to clear it away in the galley but went back to sunbathing so she could top up her tan!

This was the least of Annabel's worries as Gemma was in big trouble. David had given her a moped and at every chance she was off to see her friends, in most cases without telling anyone where she was going. The final straw was the night before when she disappeared during the evening and didn't return home until very late that night.

Annabel was standing at the front door in her dressing gown with her arms crossed waiting as Gemma tried to creep in.

"Where the fuck have you been? We were so worried we were going to call the police"

"Why are you always on my case, I was only seeing Marcus for a drink with some of his friends."

"Go to bed now and we will speak about this tomorrow, but understand you are grounded, no more going out for the next week, and if I have my way the next month."

In the morning when Annabel got up and looked outside, the small car that they used for a runabout was not parked in the drive. Where the hell was it? She went outside and saw both hers and David's cars parked but not the banger.

She went inside to tell David and to speak to the children, perhaps they knew something

"I heard a car start up during the night," said Barry "But I thought it was someone from next door."

David called the police who came around within an hour and took details. Over the next few days, the police reported that they had found the car and the man who had stolen it, which turned out to be Marcus, Gemma's boyfriend. He had told the police that he had only done it as a prank and was sorry but didn't know what all the fuss was about.

The police told David and Annabel that he had run out of fuel so when he stopped, he went into the closest house and stole some., Unfortunately the car was petrol and he had put diesel into it, which had made the car undrivable. When he tried to drive away the engine blew up, so he abandoned the car. What made matters worse was that the fuel he had stolen was from the Mayor's home and he wanted to prosecute.

Marcus was taken to the local police station and eventually prosecuted and sent to prison for several months as this was not the first time he had stolen.

Gemma was put on restricted time, no dates without telling where she was going and no boyfriends unless her parents met them first.

Barry had left school and got a job in a department store in London in the menswear department and was going to look for a place to stay with his friend Thomas from school. Thomas was working at a restaurant so the boys would always be able to eat but at the moment they didn't have enough money to rent a flat. Annabel said that they could stay at the London flat until they had saved enough money to move out.

"This is only a temporary measure to help get you on your feet. You can stay for a few months. These are the rules; don't make a mess, don't go into the office it is out of bounds, no parties and if you use the phone put some money in a box by the telephone."

Poppy wanted to study art at college and Simon was still in school for another year, the question was what to do with Gemma.

Gemma was very pretty with an outgoing personality and bags of confidence. She seemed to have an aptitude for the arts and drama and after a family discussion it was decided that she could study at the Arts Educational School in London at the end of the summer. She moved up to London and shared a flat with some friends from Portsmouth. Two bedrooms with a double bed in each, so the girls had to share a bed and the two boys in the second bedroom. David said that he would pay for this, but she had to work hard as this was a last chance for Gemma to make something of herself.

Elke by this time had returned home to Germany but kept in touch by letters and always remembered the children's birthdays with cards and small gifts.

Annabel had started recording the daytime TV programme, but she could only commit to one day a week as now that agency was really taking off, she didn't want to jeopardise her company and be away from the office for too many days.

The recordings were a lot of fun, meeting other woman who were also guests on the programme and hearing about their lives. She had spent several days at the studio getting to know the crew and felt comfortable in front of the camera as before she had married, she had appeared in some films; only small parts with few lines but it had given her a taste for showbusiness. She had an Equity card so could in the future take up this side of the business.

While David had been home, they had been out almost every evening; dinner at friends' homes, the local theatre and best of all a ball in the wardroom for the officers at Portsmouth Dockyard.

She dressed very carefully in a new ball gown that she had bought in London at a sale; she wasn't yet able to buy any of the samples from Susie that was yet to come. The dress had a tight bodice and was cut very low with a full shirt down to the ground. The material was black lace shot through with gold thread and she felt very glamorous as she entered the room where the ball was being held

A marine band was playing music on a stage that had been erected at the end of the room and everyone was either dancing or standing around talking.

David led her over to a group of officers some of which she had not met before and introduced her. She shook hands with everyone, greeted the people she knew until she came in front of a man with the most hypnotic blue eyes she had ever seen, he was tall over six feet and well-built. The air in the room seemed to have dissipated and she felt time had stood still. This was the most extraordinary feeling ever, it felt like there was electricity around the two of them, it was as if they already knew each other although they had never met before.

"Hi, I am Oliver and I am really pleased to meet you, David has told me so much about his beautiful wife that I feel I know you already."

Annabel for the first time in her life was at a loss for words but she managed to smile and say something before she moved on to speak to some friends.

The evening was fun with a four-course meal cooked by Navy chefs which was superb. Best of all Oliver was seated at their table with his wife, a pretty lady but very quiet; she did not seem to be enjoying the evening and looked cross.

After dinner they all got up to dance and Annabel was hoping that Oliver would ask her. Just before the ball ended, he did.

"Would you like to join me on the dance floor? I am sorry, but I have two left feet but if you are willing, we could try."

Annabel got up and moved into Oliver's arms, the band was playing, 'Every Breath you Take' and it felt that every breath Annabel took was hurting her heart. Being in Oliver's arms just felt so right but she knew it was a dangerous feeling.

They spoke very little, just inconsequential things; were they enjoying the evening? Had they been on holiday? nothing of any real importance. At the end of the dance Oliver lent forward and said very quietly in her ear

"I hope we meet again."

Later that night as Annabel lay in bed, she thought about Oliver and how she had felt in his arms. Would she see him again? Should she?

So many questions and no answers, she certainly would not make the first move, this was dangerous ground she could be walking into and one she had not walked before.

Chapter Ten
West Berlin

Freddie was in a buoyant mood when Annabel walked into the office the next morning.

"Hey boss, lots to tell you. Had a call from Burberry. They want to meet with you as they want a press show for their new collection and there is an audition for a new soap commercial, but they want to see kids. Have we got enough that we could send them photos of? And, the Army phoned, the producer of the Berlin Tattoo wants to speak to you about choreographing the finale this year."

Freddie sat there with a big smile on his face, perhaps the thought of all those men in uniform was giving him palpitations.

"Ok, Freddie first phone round to some of the girls on our books who have children and ask if they might be interested in the commercial and if so get them to send us in some photos asap. Next give me the phone numbers of Burberry and the Berlin producer."

"Oh, boss thought I would also mention that this morning when I came in all the files with the models contact details have been moved around and were not in the correct order."

Barry and Thomas, thought Annabel, I told them the office was out of bounds, I will speak to them this evening.

She called the press office at Burberry and was put

through to the man in charge and made an appointment to meet up to discuss what they needed. Next, she tried to call the producer of the Tattoo, but he was unavailable, but she left a message asking him to call.

Freddie and Annabel spent the rest of the morning sifting through photos of the models and identifying which of them needed to have new photos or Z-cards, answering the phone and making calls for kids that they could send for the soap commercial.

"Perhaps, Freddie we need to produce a head sheet with at least a dozen photos on, check with the printer how much this would cost and then divide the cost up between the models. I don't want to make any money on this just to have the cost covered."

The phone rang at lunchtime from Major Michael Cooper from the Tattoo office.

"My dear I have heard some very good things about you, and I wondered if you might be interested in choreographing the finale. I have just too much to do and there really isn't anyone suitable here to teach the boys how to dance."

"Dance, what are you thinking about, and would we get any volunteers to learn."

"Don't worry about volunteers, they will have their orders. I was thinking about using 500 soldiers, they would all be based in West Berlin so you would need at least a week to teach them, can you spare the time? You will also have to visit the Royal Marine headquarters in Deal to organise which piece of music you want them to play."

Annabel thought that a trip to West Berlin would be an experience, but what to do with 500 men! Major Michael arranged to meet up with her so that they could go through what was required and her fees.

"Do come with some ideas, we want the theme to be Scottish."

With that he hung up.

What about trying to make a pattern of a thistle with the soldiers in the arena thought Annabel and perhaps we could be allowed to use flaming torches, if this was allowed. She would run this idea passed Major Michael when they met up.

Gemma called before she finished for the day to tell her how she was getting on at Arts Educational.

"Hey Mum, how are things at work, anything interesting to tell me about. Can't wait till I finish here at Arts so that I can come and help you at the agency. Hear that the boys are really enjoying living in the flat especially as they have all the phone numbers of the models, and with the sizes of their busts, and they have been out on lots of dates."

Annabel knew who had been going through the files, she would put a stop to that immediately or the boys would be out on their ear. She had noticed also that the telephone box they used for calls was always empty, when she had spoken to Barry he had said that they did put in money regularly but when they got hungry they emptied the box to buy food.

She met up with the press office at Burberry's the following week and they told her that they wanted two press shows over one day for their new collections, using about 12 models which they wanted to audition before using, as they had a certain style and look they were very keen to uphold. She was also shown the showroom where the shows would be performed and the room for the models to change.

Annabel promised that she would send over a quotation for the production and if they wanted to go ahead, she would arrange the models to come in and then her stylist Charlie who would with their help select the merchandise to be used.

She telephoned both Charlie and Lindy to tell them about the proposed show as she would need both girls for the production.

Annabel had also met up with Major Michael and run by him her ideas for the finale which he loved and thought that it would be a stunning end to the Tattoo.

Arrangements had been made for Annabel to fly over to Berlin to meet everyone involved in the production and she had also found time to go to the Royal Marine Headquarters in Deal to talk about music selection.

Standing at Heathrow Airport waiting to board the flight to Berlin Annabel was excited to visit this city. She had been told that a car and driver would be waiting for her when she came through arrivals and that she would be staying with one of officers and his family. Although on this trip she was only staying a few days just to meet everyone there would be time for her to be shown the city and, if she liked, a trip across the wall could be arranged.

Arriving at West Berlin she was greeted by a solder in uniform holding up a card with her name on and after collecting her luggage she was taken to a car that had been put at her disposal for the duration of the trip

The drive through the city to the barracks was enjoyable. The city was very modern with lots of new buildings, street performers and fast-food stalls and the driver was a mine of information pointing out places of interest. One of the most fascinating stories was about the Blue Church which had been, all but destroyed during the last war but rebuilt about 1960. It had stunning blue windowpanes at each of the windows and it had been said that if you looked at the church at a certain time of day each of the windows showed a cross, which really was not possible as no crosses were in the windows — a true phenomenon.

She was taken directly to the wardroom as lunch was being served and introduced to the commanding officer. It was quite a nerve-wracking experience as Annabel was the only woman present and she didn't want to do or say anything out of place.

After lunch she was shown the parade ground where the rehearsals were to take place and then taken to the home of the officer where she would be staying.

She was greeted by Lily the officer's wife who made her very welcome introducing her to her children when they came home from school and inviting her to join them all for a family supper that evening.

The next day was backed up full of meetings with the men who would organise the 'recruits' who would be dancing, the schedule for the rehearsals was arranged and she had been told that she must keep strictly to the timetable as the soldiers had other duties and also had to have their meals at the times stated. As she would be working with such a large group of men it was decided to break them into four groups and only bring them together for the final few days

At the end of the day she was asked if she would like to have a trip across the wall to look at East Berlin as some of the men were organising an evening out.

Annabel was taken to the home where she was staying so she could change and tell Lily she was out for the evening.

A car collected her about 7pm with the group of men who she would be going out with and they seemed like a nice bunch friendly and helpful. As the approached the checkpoint at the wall where they were to cross to East Berlin they were stopped by the Russian guards and asked to show their passports, they just held them up as the guards were not allowed to handle them.

As they drove through the streets, they passed dilapidated, bullet pockmarked apartments, a very poor country as most businesses were owned and controlled by the government. Annabel was told there were limited supplies in the few restaurants and very strict laws.

The restaurant they were due to eat at was very dark and dismal but looked clean. There was a lone violin player in the corner of the room and only a very limited menu with one wine available. The food they served was good and very tasty, steak with small potatoes and perfectly done. Bread was available, but no butter and coffee were served without milk.

The evening was a great success as one of the men had brought with him his bagpipes and played many tunes which the whole restaurant seemed to enjoy.

The drive back through the wall was uneventful and she arrived back at the home she was staying in West Berlin about midnight.

Lily was waiting up for her and asked if she would like a drink before she went to bed. They sat in the lounge drinking when Lily asked Annabel if she could ask a big favour.

"Things have not been going well between my husband and I and he has just signed up for another tour of duty here in Berlin. I am not sure if I want to stay but if I go back to England, I do not know how I will manage. I have some jewellery belonging to my late mother which I could sell, and I wonder if you would take it back with you and either I or a friend will collect it in the next few months."

"Sure, no problem, just give it to me in the morning and I will pack it in my case and you can collect it the next time you are in London."

The next morning as Annabel was getting ready to leave for the airport Lily handed Annabel a very well wrapped package which she put into her case.

I didn't ask to see the jewellery thought Annabel as she was being driven to the airport, I hope it is not stolen or drugs, just my luck to be stopped at customs and be asked to unpack. Still Lily had seemed a nice woman and did not appear to be a 'drug runner' and it wasn't her place to ask too many questions. She was looking forward to her next trip over to West Berlin; a fascinating city and she had made some good friends.

Chapter Eleven
Oliver

Annabel went straight to the flat in London as David was away again and the boys had left as they had found an apartment they could afford. There was no one at home as all the children were away and she wanted to be in the office the next day.

Early the next morning Annabel was in the office sorting through the messages Freddie had left for her when the telephone rang.

"Hello, Annie's Agency, can I help you?"

"Hello Annabel, this is Oliver, we met in Portsmouth, perhaps you remember."

Annabelle's heart was racing, and she took a deep breath before she answered.

"Hi, Oliver of course I remember you, how nice to speak to you again, to what do I owe the pleasure?"

"Well, I have come up to London for an appointment which has just been cancelled and wondered if you would like to meet me for lunch, but don't worry if you are busy, I just phoned on the off-chance that you might be free."

"I am not so busy that I can't get away, how about 1pm, if that is OK."

After arranging a place to meet not far from the office they hung up. Annabel just sat thinking about Oliver, what had she done? Was this a good thing? Where might it lead? But she was excited to see Oliver again and to hell with the consequences.

She spent a busy morning when Freddie came in but found time to change and redo her makeup.

"Hey boss you look good, going anywhere nice?"

"Just meeting a friend from Portsmouth for lunch and I might take the rest of the afternoon off so see you in the morning."

It was a nice day, so Annabel decided to walk to the restaurant as it wasn't far. When she opened the door of the restaurant, she looked round to see if Oliver had arrived and there he was sitting at the back of the room. As she walked towards him, he stood up and smiled. Oh, my God he was gorgeous, and Annabel's heart did a little jump.

They sat staring at each other, and you could feel the electricity in the air between them, and then both started to speak at once.

"Hey, how have you been?"

"What are you doing in London?"

Oliver ordered some wine after asking Annabel what she liked. As Annabel drunk very little, she didn't mind what was served and told Oliver to choose. They ordered their meal and then just sat for the next few hours finding out about each other and enjoying just being together.

Oliver said that he had been offered a new commission which would mean that he would be based in Hampshire for the foreseeable future, this was a promotion for him, so he was looking forward to starting the new job, and was the reason he was in London.

Annabel told him about her trip to West Berlin and how exciting it had been and about the various work she had done and what was coming up.

Time went by so quickly that when they looked up the waiters were hovering around wanting to clear their table as lunch was long since over, and they wanted to go home.

"What are you doing this afternoon? Perhaps if you are not busy, we could go for a walk or go shopping, or something else?"

Oliver's fingers had come across the table and he was holding Annabel's hand which felt so right.

Annabel looked down at their fingers entwined, "Perhaps we can do something else," she said looking straight into his blue eyes which she saw gave her the answer she was looking for.

Oliver paid the bill quickly and they left the restaurant, in the street he hailed a cab and asked the driver to take them to a hotel in Piccadilly he knew. They turned to each other as the driver pulled away from the curb and the gap between them closed as Oliver pulled Annabel into his arms and kissed her.

After Oliver had checked them into the hotel they went to their room, they didn't notice the surroundings they only had eyes for each other.

Oliver slowly undressed Annabel taking off each of her garments slowly and kissing each part of her as he did so, until she was standing in the room naked. Then he quickly took off his clothes as if he couldn't wait or waste any more time.

They fell onto the bed hardly daring to breath just wanting to devour each other. Hands and lips were everywhere, touching and kissing in every place on each other's bodies.

They explored each other, with hands, fingers, lips as if they couldn't get enough, running their fingers over each other's faces.

"Annabel, you are so beautiful, I am so lucky to be here with you, I wanted to be close to you from the first time I saw you, but I didn't think you were interested."

"Oliver, I felt the same, I wanted you too, please Oliver take me now."

He rolled Annabel onto her back and slowly put his engorged penis into the very special part of her, slowly pushing until he could go no further, but moving slowly so he could feel all of her. She raised her legs so that they were behind his neck which meant that she could take all of him inside her and feel every piece of him.

She could feel her orgasm start and a warm rush of feeling coming over all of her body, her heart was beating very quickly and her nipples were erect when his lips came round them and bit with tiny little bites which hurt but made the feeling even more intense. She could feel the tension building into waves of pleasure as she climaxed into a blinding explosion just as she felt Oliver come inside her, they had reached that special place together.

They lay back onto the bed sweat cooling on their bodies and both smiling with the pleasure they had given and received.

Annabel's turned over to kiss Oliver and saw that he was smiling, and those gorgeous blue eyes crinkled up. She traced her fingers across his chest with light brushes touching every inch of him until she came to his penis which she saw even in his relaxed state was huge.

She bent over and ran her lips and tongue over him.

"Baby, not yet, I need to rest."

Annabel did not respond as she saw he was enjoying the sensation of her lips. She took him into her mouth and slowly used her tongue up and down the length of his penis until it was fully engorged and rigid. Slowly at first but as her mouth quickened, she felt him move beneath her until he climaxed into her mouth.

"That is the very best lunch I have ever had," said Oliver smiling as he took her into his arms. and they lay on the bed just relaxing in that beautiful moment after the greatest sex they had ever had. Knowing it was forbidden made it even more delicious.

Where to now? What was next? Would they see each other again? Or was this a onetime fling?

Chapter Twelve
Catching Up

Annabel's head was consumed with thoughts about Oliver and she wondered when and if she would see him again, but back to business she thought as she settled down for another day at the office.

It was so exciting not knowing what each day would bring she just loved creating ideas for productions and working on them until they came to fruition. Being in charge gave her such a sense of satisfaction much more so than when she was working in front of the camera. Even the day-time TV programme did not thrill her so much and unfortunately at the end of that summer she had to tell the producer that she really did not have the time to spend filming. He told her he was sad to see her leave as she had made a good impact on the programme. She promised to keep in touch and if anything came up that he thought might be of interest to contact her.

Annabel had been phoning all the exhibition organisers to introduce the agency and to try and make appointments to go and see them. She had heard of a small exhibition at Earls Court in London for the Ski Federation and there was a buzz about how good it was. She managed to track down the organiser Austin Peter who lived in Folkstone and was running an antique fair there.

Annabel caught a train down to Folkstone to meet up with

Austin as he said that he was busy for the next month on local shows but would very much like to talk to her about some sort of show at the Ski Show at the end of the year.

His antique fair was held in the open on a large field, not really her type of thing but interesting to look around. Fortunately, it was a fine day and the field was not too muddy. That would teach her not to wear her new high-heel shoes before asking where the show was being held.

Austin was dressed in bizarre clothing; just torn jeans, open neck shirt and a windcheater, not the type of gear you would have thought a man who was running an exhibition would wear. But he was friendly and between holding conversations with a variety of people all who wanted his attention she managed to tie him down long enough to speak about the Ski Show

"I like the idea of having ski fashion shows at the exhibition, but I would need you to contact my clients who have taken stands and sell them the idea of participating in the shows. I will fund the show but will need some contribution from the stand holders. I am not sure where we would have the stage that would depend on what space was available, but if this goes well and the paying public like the shows, we will do it again next year on a bigger scale."

"That's great Austin, how soon can you let me have a list of who will be showing the ski wear so I can start calling them? I will also let you have a quote for the show, I will just use eight dancers this time and keep the cost down."

At the end of the day Annabel was sitting on a train home just thinking about the commitments she had; The Burberry show was a go, West Berlin in November, and the Boat Show next January and now the Ski Exhibition later in the year. She had better speak to Lindy and Charlie, perhaps they could all meet up at home and go through the schedule and work out what was needed for each show. Fortunately, the shows did not clash so she could use some of her best dancers. But she must not forget to cross off the time she would be in West Berlin for the Tattoo.

Back in Portsmouth after a trying day travelling, she opened the front door to an empty house. It was so quiet without the children around, she thought that she would phone them all and see if they were free to come home for the weekend or just Sunday lunch. They all needed to catch up and be a family again.

The phone was ringing as she hung her coat in the cupboard and she just managed to pick it up before it rung off,

"Hello, it's me, who's speaking?"

"Hello me, it's Oliver, I am sorry to call so late, but this is the first time I have had a break."

"Oh, Oliver it is so nice to hear from you, I was wondering when we would speak."

Her heart was racing with just the sound of his voice which was doing all sorts of funny things to her insides.

"Annabel, I wanted you to know it was very special for me to see you yesterday. I would like to see you again, soon if possible. If you are free to have a quick lunch, I know a nice pub in the country. It is off the beaten track so would not create too much attention in case you are concerned. I have some free time on Friday if you can fit me in?"

"Yes, Oliver I can just about fit you in," said Annabel with a laugh.

Friday couldn't come soon enough, just to see Oliver again, and be close to him was all that she wanted.

She spent the next few days with the girls bringing them up to speed on all that was going on. Charlie told her that if this much work was coming in, she would put a manager in the boutique and spend her time on the shows. Lindy was just happy not to have to dance at the nightclub, which was not her life's ambition; she was a good dancer but a great choreographer.

"If you feel that you would like to audition some of the new models and dancers who have joined the agency just let me know, and we could advertise for some new people as we don't want to spread ourselves too thin."

They arranged to meet the following week when perhaps Annabel had some more information about the Burberry show and then Charlie could go to London to select the merchandise. Lindy said that she would be in touch with Dave their sound engineer to listen to some new music tracks.

She made time when she got home to phone the children and they all agreed that a Sunday lunch was just what they wanted. Poppy and Simon were home at the weekends anyway and Gemma said she could tear herself away from Arts and Barry sounded that he just wanted to have a good meal, get his washing done and perhaps get a sub from Mum as it was so expensive living in London.

Finding the pub on Friday took a while as Annabel did not know this part of the countryside and didn't want to be late as Oliver had said that he only had an hour. At last as she rounded the bend, she saw the pub. It was so pretty, thatched roof with hanging baskets outside filled with an abundance of summer flowers and sitting at a table outside waiting for her was Oliver.

She felt shy as she walked across the carpark

"Hello pretty lady, glad you found this place, let's go in and get a drink."

They entered the main bar, which was dark, with a low ceiling and just a few people sitting inside, they found a table at the back of the room and sat down beside each other.

Oh, how she wanted to touch him thought Annabel. She felt Oliver's fingers creep along the bench where they were sitting until he found her hand and crushed it in his own strong hand. Their eyes never left each other such was the hunger they both felt.

After what seemed like just a few minutes Oliver said that he had to go as he had a meeting, but an hour had passed.

He walked Annabel to her car and opened the door for her.

"I can arrange to have some more time next week if that is good for you, perhaps this time we can have a picnic."

"Yes, any day is fine with me, and don't worry I'll organise the picnic, and a rug. Just tell me where to meet you."

Oliver leant down and softly brushed his lips against hers

"Until next week. I'll phone you to arrange everything."

He turned, strode across the carpark, got in his car and drove away.

Chapter Thirteen
Problems and a Picnic

As Annabel climbed the stairs to her office, she could hear Freddie on the phone, he was talking in a very loud voice and it sounded like he was trying to placate whoever was on the end of the phone.

"Oh, darling don't cry, just come home, it sounds like you have had a terrible time. We will help you, but please just stop crying."

"Freddie what on earth is the matter? who are you talking to?"

Freddie covered the phone with his hand and told Annabel that their model Annaliese who had been booked for a job in Germany was on the phone from Munich in tears. He handed the phone to Annabel.

"Annaliese, please tell me what the matter is and how I can help."

"Annabel this job has been terrible, the boss of the company wants all the models to socialise with his clients at night. I thought it was just to have a meal together but the clients are awful they think the models are there for their benefit to have a good time. When we had finished the meal, they wanted to go to a club and as the other girls wanted to go and I did not want to be seen as a party pooper I went along, but the club was so sleezy in the worst part of Munich. When we got there, we were shown into a private room and the men started to use coke and expected us to join in, and to do other things. Annabel please I want to come home, but the boss said if I leave, he will not pay me and will blacklist me from getting any jobs in London."

"Annaliese where are you now? Have you got your passport with you?"

"I'm at the hotel and my passport is with the hotel reception, please get me on a plane to come home."

"Annaliese just sit tight, I am going to get to the bottom of this and also get you booked on the next flight. Just leave it with me."

Annabel found the phone number of the company offices in London and asked to speak to the owner of the company who she knew was not in Munich. When she was put through, she quickly explained the situation and stressed how unprofessional this was, and how she expected her model to be on the next flight home, and that all the fees she had been contracted for to be paid immediately. If this was not done, she would expose the company for the way they had treated the models throughout the industry.

The owner of the company was horrified to hear how one of his senior managers was treating the girls and he assured Annabel that the model would be flown home immediately, and full payment made. He also told her that he would investigate these allegations and report back to her.

"I will arrange for a ticket to be left at Munich airport for your girl to collect and I will also arrange for a car to collect her from London airport to drive her home. I am so sorry Annabel, this is totally unacceptable and you did the right thing in letting me know."

Annabel spent the next hour phoning Annaliese back and telling her the arrangements that had been made. She also made sure that she had enough money to get a taxi to the airport or if not to book one and charge it to the company.

"Please call me once you are back home so I can be sure you are safe, and I will call you in the morning so we can speak."

This was the first time that Annabel had experienced such a situation like this with a client of hers. She had heard that this was quite prevalent in the modelling world but had not had it happen to one of her models before and she felt quite sick at the thought of what could have happened if the girl had not called her. Well no matter how much the company apologised she would not work with them again and she would check out very carefully all new clients before she sent any models to work abroad.

Annabel had by then received confirmation from the London Ski Show and a list of the stand manufacturers at the exhibition so she could start to contact them to ask if they were interested in participating in the fashion show. She had sent off the costings for the production, keeping it quite small as she wanted to prove herself and get the contract for the following year. Now she had to concentrate on organising the picnic.

Oliver had arranged for them to meet at the pub in the country where they had a drink before. She drove into the pub carpark and Oliver was waiting in his car. He indicated for her to follow him which she did until they came to a layby next to some open fields which were surrounded by tall hedges.

They parked and Oliver helped her with the things she had brought for them; simple food, cold chicken, some tomatoes, strawberries, grapes and cheese and a bottle of wine. She also had a rug that she had found at the back of her cupboard at home.

They climbed over a stile and walked along the field behind the hedges until they came to a flat piece of land well hidden from the road and laid out the rug.

It was a beautiful hot sunny day and they could not wait to hold each other and as they sat down, they reached out until their bodies were close and they could feel the desire that they both felt.

"It's much too hot for clothes," said Oliver as he started to undress Annabel and then himself until they were naked in the hot sun. It felt so nice to be completely undressed with the sun beating down on them as they lay on their backs, eyes closed with just their fingers touching.

Annabel could feel a slight breeze on her body and when she looked, she could see Oliver just blowing small breaths over her and then she could feel his hands slowly touching each part of her just lightly as if they had all the time in the world. She could feel his hands growing more insistent as they investigated all the parts of her; her face, her lips, her breasts and then they came around her so he could cup her bottom in his large hands. His fingers were exploring the crevasse in her bottom and then his fingers were inside, moving very slowly until she could feel the heat in her start to rise, touching each and every part of her body. She wanted him so badly, she wanted him quickly now, she wanted to feel his hard penis inside her, his warmth filling her up, she wanted all of him.

"Now Oliver, please now, fuck me."

Oliver arranged his body above her and looked deeply into her eyes as he slowly entered her. She was wet with just the thought of his male hardness inside her and they quickly came together in a wild orgasm.

They lay that way until she felt him slowly leave that special part of her.

"Now we have had the starter shall we go for the second course, what have you brought me to eat?"

Annabel opened the picnic and gave him pieces of chicken and tomato, while Oliver opened the wine which tasted quite different here in the open air. When they had drunk a glass of wine, Annabel fed him strawberries, which felt quite sexy as his mouth closed over her fingers and sucked on them, one finger at a time. She just could not get enough of this fabulous man. Every look, every touch did something to her insides. Sex had never been this good before, not with anyone, ever.

They sat awhile just talking and kissing until it was time to go. They got dressed and cleared up the food they had left.

Oliver carried the rug and bag with the remains of the picnic. He climbed over the stile and picked her up in his arms until she was clear and then gently put her down.

"That is the very best picnic I have ever had," smiled Oliver

"I'll call you tomorrow."

They walked slowly back to their cars and kissed as they said goodbye and drove away from the beautiful afternoon they had shared.

Chapter Fourteen
Spring Cottage

Annabel was on her way to meet a client at Spring Cottage at Cliveden, the former home of Viscount Astor and where the start of the Profumo Affair had begun. The client was going to hire the cottage for a press launch and wanted Annabel's opinion on the suitability of the venue due to its notoriety during the early 1960s.

On arrival at Spring Cottage Annabel was taken aback by how pretty the cottage was, surrounded by a private flowered English garden with a half-timbered façade and a covered porch leading to the front door, which was open, so she went in.

"Hello, is anyone at home?"

A smartly dressed man came to greet her; he must have been in his early fifties with dark, curly hair greying at the temples, but he had a warm smile and held out his hand to greet her.

"Hello, I am Jack and welcome to Spring Cottage. Let me give you a tour of the place. It is quite something."

They walked together into the main sitting room which was empty of furniture but bright with sunlight. At the front of the room were windows looking onto the front garden where Annabel had just come. The windows were hung on each side with heavy brocade curtains. At the back of the room were

French doors leading out to a garden and then a path which led down to the swimming pool which Annabel could see in the distance. But the most engaging feature was an enormous fireplace where at least six men could stand, it was heavily moulded on either side of the fire opening and had a mantle shelf, above which was hung a very heavy gilt mirror

"Come and stand inside, I want to show you something."

Annabel moved into the fireplace opening which had quite an eerie feel about it.

"Watch this," Jack pulled a lever at the side and the back wall of the fire grate moved slowly back to reveal another room hidden behind glass. There was a large four poster bed inside.

"Come with me and I will show you how special that room is"

Jack held out his hand which Annabel took lightly in hers and he pulled her to walk with him through the sitting room and out to the hall where he opened a door which led into the bedroom they had just seen through the glass. The bedroom walls were hung with wallpaper with a busy pattern, all swills and lines but when you looked closely you could see that the pattern showed men and women engaged in all forms of sexual intercourse. Opposite the bed the whole wall was mirrored, so anyone in bed could watch themselves making love.

When Annabel looked at the ceiling, she could see that there was a mirror above the bed too.

"If you are in the room above you can see straight into this bedroom, so with the fireplace and room above it must have provided some exciting entertainment," said Jack smiling. "Many of the bedrooms have the same setup, and if you remember this was the home of Cliveden's resident osteopath

Stephen Ward, so there must have been some fun parties going on here at that time."

Annabel had heard stories about the parties and how John Profumo had met Christine Keeler at one of them here at the cottage.

"Want to try it out?"

Annabel looked at Jack. Should she answer that question? She certainly did not want to have an embarrassing situation arise, but to totally ignore him was not a good idea. She needed to make sure that this client understood that this was work.

"No, thank you, Jack. I don't think my husband would be very pleased. Can I see the rest of the cottage and then perhaps you can give me some idea of your press day, and what you want to achieve?"

They spent the next hour or so going over the details of the product launch and Annabel suggested that the promotional staff that she would supply would be dressed in outfits from the 60s with hair and makeup from that era.

At the end of the meeting she held out her hand to say goodbye to Jack but instead of taking her hand he pulled her close to him, just a little too close for Annabel's liking and bent down and kissed her on the lips. Annabel pulled away.

"I think that was uncalled for."

"I am sorry Annabel, perhaps I read the wrong signals. I thought you might be interested. You are so beautiful I just wanted to be close to you."

"No, Jack there were no signals and I am not interested. I will send you a quote in the post and if you want to go ahead just let me know."

With that Annabel turned and left the cottage.

Why did men think that any girl was fair game thought

Annabel as she drove away, she would inflate the cost of the product launch and If he wanted to still go ahead, she would book a manager to oversee the day. Bloody men!

Chapter Fifteen
Poppy

Today was the day Annabel was going to go through the accounts to make sure that all invoices had been sent out, check which ones had been paid and send out cheques to the staff. Most importantly she needed to chase any late payers.

There was one company in London for whom the agency had produced a fashion show last month, they had paid the 50% upfront but she was still waiting for the balance to be paid. She had chased the owner of the company many times sending out letters, making calls all of which had been ignored so today was the day for some action. She was going to give them one last chance.

"Good Morning, this is the Annie's Model Agency, can I please speak to the owner or whoever does the accounts as I am chasing a very overdue payment."

"I am so sorry, but the owner is unavailable at the moment and the lady who does the accounts is away ill."

Annabel hung up, no more excuses she was going to take some action. She left Freddie in the office and took a taxi to the showroom.

When she entered the building, she went straight to the offices at the back., She introduced herself to the lady sitting at the desk and explained why she was there.

"I need to collect a cheque for the overdue payment for

the fashion show we organised last month, who do I see?"

"I am sorry but everybody is busy with meetings or seeing clients so you will have to make an appointment."

"No, that will not be necessary. I will just wait here, all day if necessary until I can be paid."

With that Annabel sat down outside the MD's office. She heard the receptionist on the phone telling her boss that she was here.

"I am sorry, but he is just too busy to see you today, you will have to come back."

Annabel did not move; the time was now 10 a.m. she had bought a magazine with her so she would not get bored. All morning people were going in and out of the office, but the owner was obviously not going to show his face. Lunch time came and went, and Annabel was still outside the door, she didn't want to move in case he left, she was not going to leave until she had a cheque in her hand.

"You can go in now."

Annabel open the door to see a very embarrassed man sitting behind his desk, he started to make excuses as to why the payment had not been made but promised he would sort it out by the end of the week.

"No, I leave here today with a cheque in my hand, or I will just stay in your showroom and speak to your clients to pass the time."

With that he opened a drawer in his desk, took out a cheque book and wrote one for the balance which he handed to Annabel.

"I am sorry to take such extreme measures, but we worked hard for your company and expected to be paid in full and on time. Let me just say that if this cheque is not met, I shall not be calling again but will see you in court, and then you will have to pay for all the extra costs involved in a court case."

Annabel put the cheque into her bag and without saying goodbye left the office. She went straight to nearest branch of her bank and put the cheque in on a special clearance. Although it would cost extra to clear the cheque it would mean that the funds would be available within one working day. She then took a taxi back to the office as she needed to catch up with the work she had not finished.

Freddie was busy on the telephone when she got back so she went straight into her own office and saw that Freddie had written the cheques for payments owed to the models on her desk ready for her signature. There was also a list of messages that had come in.

On looking through the she saw that one was from Charlie's husband. I wonder what he wants, she thought, I hope it isn't a problem with Charlie. She dialled his number and he answered after a few rings.

"Hi Annabel, thank you for calling me back, this is rather embarrassing but as you have been so good with Charlie, I thought that I would speak to you and let you know what I heard. A friend of mine runs a detective agency and he was given an assignment to follow an officer in the navy in Portsmouth."

Annabel went cold, she could hardly catch her breath, but she needed to hear the rest of the story.

"It appears that when the detective was following the man, he saw him with you in a pub having a drink, now this might be quite innocent, but I thought that you should know."

Annabel did not make any comment just thanked Charlie's husband for the call and hung up.

She thought that she should tell Oliver and ask him what she should do. She did not want to call him at the base, so would have to wait until he contacted her.

In the meantime, she had to be very careful. She was so worried and upset never having been in a situation like this, a detective following her. It made her feel sick and really uncomfortable that someone might be spying on her, watching what she was doing and who she was seeing, although the assignment was not on her she had been seen having a drink with a man who was not her husband. What would David say if he heard, how would she explain? So many questions and no answers.

Annabel could not concentrate on work she desperately needed to speak to Oliver. Who on earth had asked a detective to follow him, and why? Was it his wife? Did she suspect that he was having an affair and was trying to find some incriminating evidence?

She finished signing the cheques ready to post but could not stay at the office and think about work. She would go home and try and work this out and hope that Oliver would contact her.

She caught a tube back to Waterloo station as she did not want to be alone but in a crowd of people. She boarded the tube but kept looking over her shoulder to see if there was any strange man watching her. Every person on the tube was suspect, she didn't know if she should look directly at the passengers or not make eye contact. She couldn't keep still, just wanted to keep moving so as soon as the tube arrived at Waterloo she quickly got off and hurried along the platform, rushing up the escalator taking the steps two at a time, such was her panic.

As soon as she arrived home, she felt that she could breathe again, she felt safe and she would spend the evening with Poppy who was in her room studying for her exams at college.

"Mum there is something that I want to speak to you about, I am leaving college soon and I would very much like to work with children and I have read all about the Montessori method of teaching. There is an intensive course in London I could take but it is very expensive. Do you think that Dad would be willing to pay as he is paying for Gemma to be at The Arts Educational school?"

"Wow Poppy where did this idea come from? If you are in London where would you live?"

"Mum I have got it all worked out, I have spoken to Gemma and she said that I could bunk in with her friend and share the expenses at the flat. Please say yes."

"Well we must speak to you father first and if he agrees, I think that you should go for it. If this is something that you want to do you will have my full support. But Poppy you will have to work hard, no going out to parties all the time, just study to pass to become a teacher, a really good one."

Poppy flung herself across the room to hug her mother

"Mum I promise, I will make you and Dad proud of me and when I pass perhaps, I can come home and open a school."

Annabel and Poppy spent the rest of the evening talking about plans for going to London to study which was just what Annabel needed to take her mind of the problem of Oliver and the detective.

Chapter Sixteen
Holidays in the Caribbean

The day dawned bright and early, but Annabel had hardly slept as she was so worried about Oliver and couldn't wait to speak to him. She decided to stay at home today as she could make calls there just as easily as at the office. She called Freddie and told him that if any clients wanted to speak to her to give them her home number.

She spent the morning doing some household duties which she had sadly neglected over the last few weeks and then went into the room she used as her office and called Freddie to find out what was happening at the office in London.

"Not much Annabel but you did have a call from The World Travel Awards. I was just going to call you and give you their number. They want at least 30 promotional staff for the exhibition."

Annabel called the company and was put through to the Managing Director.

"Thank you, Annabel, for calling me back, as explained to your booker we need promotional staff for the various companies who have resorts based around the world. The girls would need to be very attractive and if they can speak a second language so much the better but not essential. They need to work the exhibition hours 10 a.m.-8 p.m. with of course breaks. The exhibition runs for three days but the girls need to come in for a briefing the day before it opens. They won't be paid but will receive a week's free holiday at one of the resorts in the Caribbean; flights, transfers, hotel and all meals each day. Can you help and do you think your girls would be interested?"

"Well that is the most unique booking I have ever been asked to organise, but I am sure that I can find you 30 girls. The question I need to ask is how will I benefit as I usually receive commission on each job that we organise."

"That is no problem as you will receive a free holiday for you and your partner or husband for 10 days at a resort of your choosing. I will leave it with you, but can you come back to me within two days and confirm that you have all the staff we need. I will need to see photographs of the girls so perhaps we can arrange to meet up and go through the details."

After Annabel had hung up, she quickly called Freddie and told him that together they needed to find the most attractive girls on their books who were willing to work in exchange for a free holiday to the Caribbean.

"Pity I am not a young pretty girl," said Freddie with a sigh "Just a gorgeous, young man"

They made up a list and divided the names up between them and arranged to speak at the end of the day before they decided who would be asked.

Annabel called all the names on her list and the girls that she spoke to said that they would like to be considered, as a holiday was just what they needed. A few were not available as they had work commitments during the exhibition dates. By the end of the day when she spoke to Freddie, they had already 35 names with at least five more still to speak to. She asked

Freddie to pull out photographs of the girls so that when she went to the meeting there would be a choice. Wait till she told David that they would be going to the Caribbean on a free holiday.

Still no call from Oliver, perhaps he would call her tonight. She was desperate to speak to him and ask what they should do, if anything but at least Oliver would be aware of the situation. Whatever happened they would have to be careful where they met, so no more pubs locally.

Annabel went to the London office the next day and spent the whole of the journey up to Waterloo wondering if there was someone watching her. She felt so uncomfortable as if something was crawling under her skin. She did not want to stop seeing Oliver but could not live like this. She thought of calling Charlie's husband back to find the name of the detective and call him, but that was not a good idea as she did not want to bring any more attention to herself. She must just wait until Oliver called, so together, they could decide what to do.

By the middle of the morning they had 38 girls on the list for the World Travel Awards exhibition and all the photos ready to show so Annabel telephoned the travel awards office to confirm when would be convenient to meet up. The managing director said that he had a gap that afternoon and if it was OK could Annabel come up to see him. He gave her his office address which was in the east end of London.

When Annabel found the offices, she rang the entry phone, announced who she was and who she was here to see, and was told to come up to the first floor

The offices were laid out with many desks all who had someone sat at them either answering the phones which were ringing constantly or running around with files under their arms. She was shown into the MD's office, but he was on the telephone and indicated for her to sit down on the only chair that wasn't covered in paper. His call was taking forever so Annabel looked around. The office walls were covered in posters all showing the upcoming exhibition and the awards that were going to be won for 'excellence in the tourism industry.'

"Sorry Annabel for keeping you waiting but it is mad here at the moment. We had a company that we thought were going to provide the promotional staff, but they have let us down and your name came up when I was talking to someone who had used you before. They gave your agency a glowing recommendation, so I am so pleased that you are able to help at such short notice."

He then went through the photographs that Annabel had brought with her and chose the 30 girls he felt were the best suited, also choosing a couple of reserves.

"Before I can book anyone I will need a contract from you on your company headed paper stating exactly what the duties of each girl are; dates, times and venue and what they will receive in return, listing just what you told me flights, hotels, transfers and full board to the resort in the Caribbean, also listing what hotel and resort each girl will be staying at."

"That is no problem, each room booked needs to be shared by two girls, but there is a window of at least three weeks when they can take the free holiday, but we cannot change the dates they must be taken within that time frame and no money will be given in exchange."

Annabel thought that all sounded fine and she was pleased to hear that he was so organised. She had done some investigating herself just to find out about the awards and the company and she had been told that the Travel Awards had been running for several years and that this was how they paid the staff. They discussed what the girls should wear, and Annabel suggested just black skirts and a smart top with high heel shoes and the stand would provide each promotional girl with a sash that had to be worn when she was on duty. He said that the contract would be with her the following day and Annabel promised that as soon as she received it, she would book the staff and would also be at the exhibition herself to make sure that the promotion was running smoothly.

It was late so she decided to go back home instead of calling into the office. She would call Freddie in the morning to check when he received the contract so that they could book the staff and send a copy out to each girl which they would have to sign and return.

Poppy was in her room with a friend when Annabel got home, so she just put her head round the door to say hello and that she was back and did the girls want anything to eat. After she had made a meal for the girls, she decided to have a bath and climb into bed with a book. After the bath she heard the phone ringing and in case it was Oliver she took the call in her bedroom and closed the door.

"Hello, Annabel speaking."

"Hey, it's me, sorry I have not called before, but it has been so busy, and I wanted to be able to speak to without any interruptions."

On hearing Oliver's voice Annabel just burst into tears.

"Annabel what is wrong? Why are you crying? Please talk to me."

Annabel stopped crying and told Oliver about the

conversation she had had and that there was a detective watching him and that they had been seen having a drink in the country.

"Annabel please stop worrying it might just be something to do with my work. I am sure that my wife has no idea that I am seeing someone, she would not care anyway, things are not great between us. We each do our own thing; she really doesn't care about me. She is so wrapped up with her charity work she has little time for anything else.

"But the detective told Charlie's husband that we were seen together, what could that mean, and why did he mention that had seen us out."

"Annabel, I am sure that this is just someone being spiteful. Let me look into it, but please stop worrying. I think that perhaps pubs are out for the moment. I will come up to London so we can have lunch together and perhaps something else!"

Annabel dried her tears and was smiling as she finished speaking, just to have someone to confide in really did help, and she had a lunch date in London to look forward to.

Chapter Seventeen
Dating a Prince

Several weeks had gone by and she had not heard any more about the detective following Oliver so she hoped that it would just go away. She and Oliver had met up in London and had spent a lovely day together but were a little more careful about meeting up at home.

Business was flourishing with many job assignments coming in for the models and the contract for the Travel Awards had been received and copies had been sent out to all the girls which were now signed and back at the office.

She had heard a rumour that one of the agency's dancers was going out with a prince. She asked Freddie who seemed to know everything that was going on and he told her that as far as he knew it was true.

"The prince is so gorgeous I wish he preferred boys, as I am available," said Freddie with a big smile. "Annabel, talking about boys, why don't you join me next weekend as there is a big party on for Gay Pride - for the lesbian, gay, bisexual and transgender community. They come together for a month-long celebration of love. I am sure that you would have fun and quite a lot of our male dancers will be going."

After Annabel had stopped laughing as she could just see herself in a parade with flamboyant guys all dressed up and strutting around, she told Freddie that it sounded like fun, but she had to be home that weekend.

"You will have to tell me all about it next week, but please be careful and don't pick up any strange men."

With that all the telephones started to ring and they both picked up the calls.

"Annie's Agency, can I help you?"

"This is the Daily Mail here can you please give us a comment about your dancer Catherine who is going out with one of the Queen's sons?"

"No thank you." Annabel hung up only for the telephone to ring again.

"Hello, this is the Daily Sketch; would you like to give us a story about your dancer going out with a prince?"

The next few hours Freddie and Annabel were taking calls from all the newspapers and some of the magazines which they both declined to answer with anything but "no thanks, no comment". In the end they took the phones off the hook just to get some respite.

In the afternoon, Catherine, the dancer in question called to speak to Annabel.

"Annabel, please don't give out any statements to any of the press, they are driving me mad. I have only been out for a few dates and the newspapers want to report a forthcoming marriage."

"Don't worry they will not be hearing anything from us, we 'gypsies' must stick together."

"What does that mean?" asked Freddie, "Gypsies must stick together, refers to a group of dancers" said Annabel, "who travel around from one job to another."

Every other call that day was from one newspaper or another who wanted some low down on the girl going out with the prince, so little work seemed to get done.

Annabel stayed over at the London flat that night and had arranged to meet up with Barry and his friend Thomas for a meal. They said they would pay for it, but Annabel knew that when the bill came, she would pick it up as they were still earning low wages and a grand gesture of paying by them was out of the question.

"Mum, I am enjoying working in London, but I do not want to make my career working in the menswear department for ever. Perhaps at the end of the summer I can look for something else to do. I quite like the idea of working in an estate agency, and if I come home, I could move back in with you to keep you from getting lonely with Dad being away so much of the time."

Annabel smiled at this comment, but she did not think Barry was that concerned about her. They spoke about the various options that could be available and Barry said that he would contact some offices in Portsmouth. Thomas, his friend said that he was doing well at the restaurant he was working at, but he was also thinking about moving on and he quite liked the idea of working in the city for a trading company, so he would have to move as well.

"Perhaps Barry if you do move back, we could convert the barn at home into your private rooms, so you would have your own sleeping and living space to entertain, that would give you some privacy and you would not be under our feet."

Barry just grinned, a perfect solution for him, back home with his private room, no rent to pay and Mum cooking his meals and doing his washing. A good result.

That night while Annabel was sleeping the telephone started to ring, she looked at the clock and it showed midnight.

Who on earth could be calling at this hour?

"Hello, who is this?"

"Daily Mail here, we spoke to you earlier in the day and asked if you would comment on the story about your dancer and the prince. I have spoken to my editor and he has said that he would pay you £1000 if you would agree to give an interview."

"No," said Annabel and hung up only for the phone to ring again.

"Daily Mail here again, I have been authorised to increase the offer to £2000, and we promise to print only what you tell us, but we do need some photographs of Catherine when she was working and any others that you might have."

"No, thank you," and hung up again.

This went on until 4am and the offer was increased each time but there was no way that Annabel would agree to give an interview so in the end she took the phone off the hook so she could get some sleep.

She was telling Freddie the next morning about the calls she had received during the night and the one-word answer that she had given each time.

Later that morning Catherine rang.

"Thank you, Annabel, for not agreeing for an interview but unfortunately my last boyfriend wasn't so nice and he accepted a fee and I understand that he has given both a story and let the newspapers have some private photographs of us on holiday. I am so upset but there is nothing I can do."

"Catherine you just have to sit tight and not let the newspapers hound you. If it's getting too much phone the editor of each paper and tell them to stop this harassment or you will get a lawyer to put an injunction on them. I do not know if this would work but it is worth a try."

Later that afternoon Freddie went out to buy the Evening Standard to see if anything had been reported and sure enough big headlines stating that Dancer was going out with a Prince. All written by the ex-boyfriend and with photos. What a bastard. The ex was also on the agency books so Annabel put all his photos in the bin with the rest of the rubbish. She would not be using him again and she very much doubted that any other reputable agency would either.

Chapter Eighteen
The Scam

The morning was busy handling various bookings when a call came in from Charlie's husband. Annabel's heart was beating fast, what on earth did he want?

"So sorry to bother you again but I have heard from my friend and he has passed on a message for you to say that if you want him to stop following any more lines of enquiries he needs to be paid for the work he will miss out on, and will accept a one off payment of £3000."

"Steve this is outrageous, the man is following a friend of mine, a naval officer. Why is he asking money from me, I am not the person in question that he was given the assignment for."

"Annabel, I am just passing on a message. I told you that I am only doing this because you are a good friend of Charlie's and I thought that you would not like your husband to hear about any of this. He has assured me that he will stop immediately but he needs to be paid in cash within five days."

After Annabel had told Steve that she would call him back the following day, she sat back in her chair with a big sigh. She needed to speak to Oliver and ask if he could help as she did not have all the money available and what assurances did she have that she wouldn't be asked again for more money at some later date, this could go on for many months and if a time came when she could not pay any more would the man go to David and tell him what was going on. It all seemed very strange that Steve should be contacting her demanding money, it felt like blackmail and before she spoke to Oliver, she wanted to do some investigations herself.

She telephoned Charlie on the pretence of meeting up with her for a discussion on the Ski Show Exhibition. She would not tell her anything about the phone call she had had from Steve but perhaps she could find out some more information, like did they have a friend who ran a detective agency and what business was Steve involved in at the moment and most importantly was he hard up for cash?

The next morning Annabel was sitting in Charlie's home going through the details that Annabel had to date on the Ski Show manufacturers that wanted to show their clothes in the fashion show.

"I still have to confirm which dancers we will be using but perhaps you can make contact with the clients and ask them to perhaps send you through some photos at this stage so at least you have some idea on what you will use, and then perhaps we can then involve Lindy to suggest music for each scene."

"That is fine, I can at least start the ball rolling so the show does not creep up on us at the last minute."

Charlie was looking uncomfortable not at all like the calm and happy person she always appeared to be, Annabel asked was anything the matter

"Annabel I really did not want to have to ask you but Steve's business is not so good at the moment and bills are coming at us from every direction. Hopefully business will pick up soon but it is really slow and I wondered if I could ask you for a loan against the next payment you will owe me. I really did not want to have to do this but I have nowhere else to turn and we have just paid out for our daughter Jessie's wedding so that has been even more expense."

"Charlie don't worry that is not a problem how much do you need."

"£500 would be great if you can and thank you for being such a good friend, I really appreciate it. Perhaps if you have the time would you like to look through the photos of Jessie's honeymoon."

Charlie went off to make another drink while Annabel looked through the photograph album. Annabel now knew who was blackmailing her and why. Steve was in trouble and thought that she could help him out, but instead of asking for a loan he had decided to take this route.

While Annabel thought this through, she flipped through the photos of Jessie, Steve's and Charlie's daughter. She knew her, as Jessie had helped as a dresser on one of the fashion shows. She came to some photos of Jessie looking very glamorous in some stunning swimwear, just like the swimwear that had gone missing from the show.

Annabel now knew what she had to do; it had all become very clear. She would not mention any of this to Charlie who was a nice decent woman. But between a blackmailing husband and a daughter who was a thief she had enough to contend with.

When Annabel left Charlie's home, she thought that she would not contact Steve just then, let him stew for another day, she would make arrangements for him to meet her in London at the office, why make things easy.

Steve was shown into Annabel's office looking very much the man about town and very pleased with himself.

"Can I offer you a drink."

"No thanks I don't have a great deal of time, I just want to conclude our business and then be on my way."

Annabel thought that she would string it out for a bit, she didn't want to give Steve an easy ride.

"Steve this has come as a big shock to me, I have never found myself in this situation before and trying to find £3000 is no easy task. What concerns me is that once I pay who is to say that I will not be asked again for more money in a few months' time?"

"Oh, don't worry your little head about that, I will make sure that you are never bothered again."

"But what guarantee do I have? It is just your word that I won't be, which is really not good enough."

Annabel could see Steve was getting hot and was not happy as to the way things were progressing.

"Look Annabel I have come to you in good faith I am only trying to help. You wouldn't want David to hear that you were having drinks in the country with another man, would you?"

"OK, Steve we better go out so that I can withdraw the money from my bank, I will take your word that I shall never be contacted again."

"Sorry Annabel, I think I will just wait here until you return."

"No, Steve I insist you accompany me as I do not want to be walking down the Kings Road with all that money in my bag. So if you won't come with me, I cannot get the money for you today."

Steve and Annabel left the office and walked towards her branch of the bank. She could see that Steve was not at all happy. Just wait until she was inside the bank when she would tell him some news about his daughter.

As they were queuing up to see the teller, Annabel leaned over and said very quietly in Steve's ear.

"Steve perhaps you could give me some advice, I have found photographs of your daughter Jessie wearing some stolen swimwear which was taken from the last fashion show we did when she was working for me as a dresser. This was reported to the police so now that I know who took the items what do you suggest I do? Also, I think that they would be very interested when I tell them that you have been trying to blackmail me. I will just forget all this unless I ever hear from you again, or if I find that David has been bothered with any unpleasant stories."

Steve looked at Annabel with a look of pure hatred, he turned on his heels and as quickly as he could left the bank.

Chapter Nineteen
Gemma

Annabel hailed a taxi which was now taking her to the Chelsea and Westminster Hospital. She had received a call from Gemma's friend to say that Gemma had been rushed into hospital with a suspected overdose of sleeping pills. She did not know any more than this brief message so was rushing to the hospital.

The emergency department was heaving with people as Annabel made her way to the reception desk. She had to wait in line as the receptionists were handling other patients' queries. It seemed to take forever before she could give her name and ask where she could find her daughter.

Annabel was directed to a ward and told to ask there. As she entered the ward, she saw Gemma in a bed surrounded by serval doctors, all of whom seemed to be in conference.

"I'm Gemma's mother. Is she all right?"

"It's OK, please just take a deep breath. You look like you're going to pass out. Do you want to sit down?"

"No, just please tell me what has happened."

One of the doctors asked Annabel to step outside the cubicle and explained that Gemma had been rushed into hospital by ambulance after they had been informed that she had taken an overdose of what appeared to be sleeping pills. She had her stomach pumped and was now doing well but they were going to keep her in overnight just to monitor her and suggested that she has a psychiatric evaluation before she was released in the morning.

"Can I speak to her?"

"I don't think she will make much sense as she is just sleeping the affects off, but her friend who brought her in is in the waiting room, so why don't you both go and get a cup of coffee and come back in a couple of hours?"

Annabel hurried out to the waiting room and saw Gemma's friend Lucy sitting in a corner looking scared out of her mind.

"Lucy, she is going to be OK. The doctors have assured me, but they are keeping her in overnight, can you tell me what happened?"

Lucy started to cry when she was told all was OK. "Gemma seemed a bit down all evening but when I asked her if she was OK, she said she was but was going to go to bed early. I took her in a cup of tea about an hour later and found her laying across the bed, and I couldn't wake her, so I called 999. They came immediately and found an empty bottle of sleeping pills in Gemma's hand, so they took them with, and that's all I know."

Annabel took Lucy into her arms and gave her a big cuddle and tried to get her to stop crying.

"Lucy, all will be OK. But do you know why Gemma took sleeping pills? Is anything worrying her? Has she told you she has any problems?"

"I don't know anything you will have to ask Gemma when she wakes up."

Annabel took Lucy for a hot drink and then gave her money so that she could take a taxi home as it was not necessary for both to be sitting in the hospital all night.

Annabel spent the rest of the night sitting by Gemma's bed holding her hand and whispering endearments.

"Darling, I love you my darling rebellious child. What have you done? Why did you not tell me what the problem was?"

Dawn crept slowly in and the ward was starting to get busy with new patients being brought in. A nurse checked on Gemma every hour and she did not seem to be worried and as Annabel did not want to cause any fuss she just sat quietly by Gemma's bed until early in the morning Gemma opened her eyes.

"Mum what are you doing here? Where am I?"

"Darling you are in hospital. Lucy called an ambulance after she found you slumped on the bed and she couldn't wake you. Do you remember anything? Why did you take so many sleeping pills?"

"Mum, I don't want to talk about it!" And with that Gemma turned over and faced away from her mother.

A little later a nurse came in to do the obs and said that a doctor would soon to be in to see her. Also, before she could be released. The morning passed slowly until she was pronounced fit to leave but would have to be accessed by someone from the psychiatric department first.

Annabel was asked to wait outside while this was going on and after about an hour, she was asked to come back into the room.

"Gemma has a few issues which we have to deal with, but she does not want to discuss them with you now, and we have to respect her wishes. I would like to suggest that she makes an appointment to see her own doctor who will refer her to a mental health specialist."

Gemma was given some notes to take to her doctor and then she left the hospital.

"Please will you let me take you home to Portsmouth where I can look after you properly and build up your strength and we can make an appointment to see our doctor at home."

"No, I am staying in London with my friends. They will look after me. I don't want to see your doctor ever, and please do not discuss this with him, just take me back to my flat."

Annabel thought it worrying that she did not want to see the family doctor who had looked after her and was a nice kindly man but not wanting to upset Gemma any more she took her back to her own flat.

After Annabel had given Gemma a light meal and put her into bed she waited until Lucy came home so that she could tell her what had happened at the hospital. She tried once more to find out why Gemma had taken the sleeping pills but Gemma was adamant that she did not want to discuss it so thought that she would wait until Gemma was ready.

While she was waiting, she telephoned Gemma's school to advise them that she was ill and was not sure when she would be returning but promised that she would keep in touch.

"Gemma darling, I will leave you here with your friend if you promise me that you will contact a doctor here in London so that you can be referred to a specialist whom you can talk to about any problems. You must call me at least once a day just to let me know how you are feeling, or I am sure that Daddy will come back and collect you and bring you back to Portsmouth."

Lucy arrived home and was pleased to see Gemma back in the flat and she also promised that she would make sure that

Gemma made an appointment in the next few days.

Annabel left with a lot of misgivings, but Gemma was an adult and she couldn't force her to come home with her.

Annabel was shaking as she made her way to the station so that she could go home. She knew that she was very tired after being up all night and with the worry about her daughter she felt that she could not cope, but she knew that she must. David was away so all the children's problems were for the moment on her shoulders, so she must stay strong.

Chapter Twenty
New Office and New Flat

Gemma was doing well and had been several times to speak to a mental health specialist but still refused to tell Annabel the reason she had felt so depressed that she had felt that she wanted to end it all. Perhaps it was a cry for help and not that she wanted to end her life.

The other children were doing well; Poppy had been given the go ahead by her father to enrol on the Montessori course in London and she would be living with Gemma while she was studying which was a good thing, she might open up to her sister. Barry had found a position back in Portsmouth with a leading estate agent and was starting work with them the following month and would be living back at home in his old room until the barn could be converted for him. But the child she was so proud of was her baby Simon, who had managed to get a place at a university in London to study electronic engineering. He would be living on campus for the first year and being such an organised young man had organised everything himself.

Now she needed to concentrate on the agency as she had been sent a letter by her landlord saying that the end of her lease was up in a few months' time and they would not be renewing the leases for any of the tenants in the building as they wanted to turn the whole building into flats and so were giving her notice.

She contacted a few estate agents to ask if there were any offices coming vacant in the near future, she did not have to be in the Kings Road as clients rarely come to the office just somewhere central for the models and dancers to call into. She was told about a basement office in Manchester Street near Selfridges that sounded like it might be of interest and made an appointment to view it that afternoon.

The building in Manchester Street looked very pretty from the outside and was close to Bond Street station which was good for models visiting. She rang the doorbell and after a few minutes it was opened by a very small elderly lady who introduced herself as Lottie, the owner of the building

"Come in my dear, I hear that you are interested in renting the basement rooms to run your modelling agency from. If you don't mind, I won't come down with you but here are the keys, you have a good look round and when you have finished come and find me. I will be in my studio here on the first floor."

Annabel climbed down the stairs which were quite narrow and opened the first of the doors which was the room nearest to the street and saw that is was bright and spacious and would be ideal. The second room at the back was smaller which would be suitable for her but was dark as it had no natural light. After studying the area Annabel thought that if Lottie would give permission, she would knock through to the room at the back to make a large open plan office suite.

After locking the rooms up, she checked where the toilet and kitchen were, and both were suitable, so she went to find Lottie to negotiate on the price for the rent as Annabel felt it was a little high for a basement.

Lottie agreed and permission was given for the alterations

and a slightly lower price for the rent with a month free for the work to be done.

"I have been running keep fit classes for the whole of my life and although I don't teach anymore, I like to keep my eye on things, so I am here most every day. I have also written a book on how to keep fit and healthy, let me give you a copy."

Annabel was happy that she had found an office which would work well and was not too far for Freddie to travel to each day. Now she had to address the question of a flat as obviously she could not use the rooms to sleep in as there was not enough space, she had been spoilt with her first office and the use of a flat. Gemma had told her that a friend was living in a beautiful flat in Baker Street which was only a few minutes away and the flat was rent controlled, and she could easily get Annabel put on the lease. It sounded ideal and if it worked out, she would have a new office and an apartment which she needed as she spent so much time in London and did not want to be travelling back and forwards to Portsmouth each day.

Now, thought Annabel, she needed a little bit of Oliver, no not a little bit but a lot! Both Oliver and she had a mobile phone, so it was so much easier to be in contact. She rung his number and was both surprised and pleased when he picked up.

Annabel told him what she had been doing that morning and how pleased she was on finding a new office space and the possibility of an apartment right in the middle of London.

"Oliver it seems like forever since I have seen you, can we meet up soon?"

"Unfortunately, I am really tied up for the next few days, but tell me what you would do if we were together now."

"Well, first of all I would undress you very slowly taking

each piece of your clothing off, I also want to tell you what I am wearing, it is your favourite suit, I shall undo the zip and let it fall on the ground and then undo the buttons of my shirt until I am standing in my underwear, the red matching set that you love so much. I am running my fingers under the bra so I can feel my nipples which are hardening as I touch them, and now I will undo it so I can feel just the air on my breasts. I have put my fingers into my pants and can feel that I am starting to get wet, just thinking about you. My fingers are stroking my vagina and are now inside, it feels so good.

"I'm brushing my lips across the back of your neck…you can feel my warm breath right between your shoulder blades, as I start lightly kissing down your spine and then stand in front of you and kiss you on every place until I come to your penis. Just small kisses then I will take you in my mouth just for a few moments, mustn't hurry I want this last a long time."

"Annabel, I want to feel your breasts I want to rub my cock on them, it feels so good, and the I want you to lay down so that I can push my cock inside of you, does that feel good darling?"

" Yes, Oliver I can now feel all of you, you feel so big inside of me, push harder, more now more."

"Oh, Annabel I am coming, wait don't move I can feel me spurt into you. Oh God, that was fantastic, what are you doing to me? I just can't get enough of you."

Annabel could hear Oliver grunt and there was silence for a few moments until she could hear him get his breath back.

"Oliver was that good, just a prelude of what we will do when we meet, tell me where you are."

"Annabel I am sitting at my desk in my office and this could have been the most embarrassing moment of my life if anyone had come in, but everyone is out at the moment so your timing was perfect," he said with a laugh

They arranged to meet up later in the week and Annabel hung up with a big smile on her face.

Chapter Twenty-One
Fashion Show in Portsmouth

The agency had been asked to produce a show to help raise funds for the children's charity The Variety Club of Great Britain. The Charity was started in 1928 in a movie theatre in America where a month-old baby was found abandoned. A note was pinned to the baby girl's dress:

Please take care of my baby, her name is Catherine. I can no longer take care of her as I have eight other children and I have always heard of the generosity of people in showbusiness and I pray to God that you will look after her

The Variety Club members took the decision to oversee the baby's upbringing and education and from one child an international charity grew and spread across the world.

Annabel was delighted to have been asked by the man in charge, 'The Chief Barker' and she was sure that all the models who were available would work for only a small fee so that all the funds raised on the sale of the tickets would be given to The Variety Club. First of all, she contacted banqueting rooms in Portsmouth to see if they would be willing to hire them out at little or no cost, but told them that it would generate much publicity for them as many famous show business personalities would attend the evening. Once she had the confirmation that the rooms could be used for the production of the fashion show, she then telephoned a few major companies in Portsmouth to ask if they would sponsor the show as there were costs involved that would have to be met. She then asked Freddie to contact at least 20 models to ask if they would be interested in being part of this special event, but to understand that the fee would not be their usual and the agency would not be taking any commission. Charlie said that she would style the show and would give her time free as the publicity for her to use the merchandise from her boutique would be good for her business,

Lindy was asked to choreograph the show and her fee, the models, and sound engineer could all be paid from the sponsorship Annabel had raised.

After a month all was organised and the Variety Club had sent a list of which celebrities would attend the evening. She contacted the local newspaper to make sure that the event would be covered, and they promised to run an advert in the paper telling everyone about the evening. Annabel had also printed posters which many of the stores and shops in Portsmouth would display telling where to purchase tickets.

The day of the show arrived, and the dress rehearsal had gone really well. Annabel had arranged for food to be delivered to the hall so that before the show everyone involved would be able to relax and have a meal. As she was sitting down and taking a breather Lindy came over to her and asked if she could speak to her privately as there was a problem.

"I have been asked by the models to speak to you as they feel that they are not being paid enough and unless you agree to increase their fee they will not perform."

Annabel was absolutely flabbergasted. She had never been held to ransom like this before. All the models had been asked if they would be part of the show and they knew exactly how much they would be paid, and Annabel had also covered the models expenses herself. She stormed off to the dressing room where the models were sitting around eating but looked up when Annabel entered.

"I cannot believe what Lindy has just told me; you all should be ashamed of yourselves. You know that this evening is to raise funds for disadvantaged children, and you all agreed to be part of it. What I am now being told is that you want to pull out. What do you want me to do? Put a poster up in the front of the building saying that the evening is now cancelled and what shall I tell the Variety Club. I am sure that the newspapers would love this story to print."

There was a lot of murmuring amongst the models until one of them spoke up.

"Lindy said that we should talk to you, we were always going to do the show, but she said you might pay us some more money if we asked."

There was silence as they looked at each other and Annabel saw that Lindy was crying so she walked over to her.

"Lindy what is this all about? Why did you stir up trouble like this?"

"Annabel all I wanted to ask is if we could be paid anymore but when I started speaking it all came out wrong. I'm so sorry I didn't want to cause any trouble and of course we are going to do the show, I'm so sorry."

Annabel turned to the room and asked each model in turn what they wanted to do. Each person said yes and that they were sorry to have caused any trouble, they didn't really mean it, just wanted to ask if the pay could be increased.

After all the models had agreed she went out to the front and sat down. This was something she would have to deal with, she couldn't go on if Lindy was going to accost her at each show and although most of the models were local, she would have to think very carefully about booking any of them again.

The show was an amazing success, the hall was fully booked so they had made a lot of money for the charity. As she went on stage to take a bow, she looked to the side of the stage and saw both Charlie and Lindy standing in the wings, so she called them onto the stage to be with her. The Chief Barker then went onto the stage, called upon some of the celebrities who had attended and took the microphone from Annabel.

"I want to thank all of the models, Annabel the agency owner and our compere for this evening, Charlie for the wonderful selection of clothes and Lindy for the choreography and in fact everyone who has been involved in this evening and most importantly to thank you the audience for helping to raise enough money to buy a new mini bus to take the children out. The bus will have our thanks on the side saying that it was presented by Annie's Agency," he then sat down to tremendous applause.

Annabel went backstage to thank everyone and all the models in turn came up to her to say how sorry they were and to thank Annabel for including them in the show.

Annabel just smiled and gave them all a cuddle, she did not want to speak about this anymore. The main point of the show was to raise money and this they had done in bucket loads.

The next day the local paper ran a two-page spread with photographs of the fashion show and the celebrities and a wonderful write-up. Annabel made a mental note that when she sent the fee to each of the models who had taken part, she would include a copy of the newspaper, and she hoped that they would think twice before anything like the deputation they had staged would be done again.

Chapter Twenty-Two
Berlin Tattoo

Annabel had just boarded the flight to West Berlin as she was needed for rehearsals at the Tattoo, and as she was going to stay over for the first day before she flew back to London she would be away for the best part of a week. The stewardesses came over to make sure everything was OK and told Annabel that she had heard she was working at the base choreographing the finale.

"My boyfriend is one of the officers and told me that you would be on this flight. Do hope all goes well but if you get bored one evening why not give me a call as I have a layover for a few days and we are going out for a meal with some of the flight crew and the boys from traffic control. It always is a lot of fun so if you can do join us that would be great." With that, she handed Annabel a note with her name and phone number.

"I would love to; I promise that if the people I am working for do not need me I will definitely join you."

A car as before was waiting for her when she arrived, and this time took her to the hotel that she would be staying at. She hoped to catch up with Lily the Officer's wife that she had stayed with on her previous trip. A friend of Lily's had collected the parcel from London that Lily had given her for safe keeping, and she wanted to find out that all was well with her.

The hotel was very basic but clean and as Annabel was going to be out every day teaching the men she did not mind as she thought that by the time she returned each night, she would just be too tried to do much but have a snack and fall into bed.

Early the next morning a car and driver arrived to collect her and gave Annabel a detailed list of where she had to be for training and also the breaks she had to adhere to as the men were expected to carry out their other duties and had set times for their meals.

All the recruits she was training were waiting for her on the parade ground ready for their first lesson. They had been broken up into several groups as it was suggested that it would be easier to train that way.

Oh gosh, thought Annabel, I really hope that they listen to me, but first she explained to the Sergeant who was in charge what she needed and showed him a few simple steps that she wanted the men to learn. He barked the instructions to the men and then a shambolic mess occurred as the men tried to follow what they had been told to do, they were going everywhere and bumping into one another.

"Sergeant Smith, I think it would be better if I showed just a few men and then when they understand the steps, they could in turn teach the others."

Annabel then showed the very simple steps that she needed the men to learn and suggested that they broke into groups to teach. After half an hour when Annabel thought that what they were doing looked more like dance steps and not a war, she stood at one end of the parade ground and shouted in a very loud voice.

"OK let us get into a circle round the parade ground and on my count start to move forward using the steps." It was a horrific sight and she was sure that the men were playing her up, bumping into one another, going the wrong way, it was just horrible. Annabel need to do something drastic or the men would never listen to her. She walked into the centre of the circle and in her loudest voice shouted "STOP!"

"OK, I will tell you what I am going to do, I am going to get a coffee and when I come back, I expect to see something that resembles some steps, if not I will just give up and go back to London and you can organise this yourself." She walked off not really knowing in which direction she could find a coffee but she was not coming back until the men stopped messing around or she was just wasting her time and the Army's time and money.

After half an hour she walked back to the parade ground and was amazed to see the men in a circle performing what was quite a decent example of what see wanted.

The rest of the day went well with all the soldiers working hard and she was looking forward now to teaching the new groups as she was sure that she would not have any more trouble.

As she was leaving the base her driver asked if she would step inside the building as the commanding officer of the base wanted a quick word with her. Annabel hoped that she had not overstepped her position as she had treated the men like naughty children not enlisted men.

"Well done my dear, I hear that the men gave you a hard time this morning, but you managed to knock some sense into them. Please do tell me if there is any way that I can help you over the next few days. We are delighted to have you here and looking forward to seeing the performance in the finale."

When she got back to the hotel, she decided to call the stewardess from the flight as a night out with some fun people was just what she felt like. They arranged to meet at a local pub at 9 p.m., which sounded quite late for Annabel, but she assumed that that the flight crew were working until then.

The pub was small, cosy, and warm and every inch of the walls were covered with an amazing array of German artefacts, it was also very noisy with people talking and loud music blaring from speakers and it was difficult to find her friend from the flight. At the back of the pub she spotted someone waving to her so walked over.

"Hi Annabel, thank you for joining us. Let me introduce everyone." She went around the table saying each person's name and what their job was, it was just too many people for Annabel to remember so she just smiled and said hello to everyone.

All the crowd were drinking what appeared to be beer out of different glasses and she was told that the Kolsch needed to be drunk out of a slender glass while the Heiewizen is served in a half litre glass with a bulge. What would you like she was asked "Anything that you recommend?"

There was also German sausage on the table, Kartoffelpuffer, which she was told was potato pancakes, a huge selection of cheese and cold meats, rye breads and an enormous dish of pretzels; enough to feed an army or the crew of the plane.

When she had eaten and drunk as much as she could manage, she spoke to the man who was sitting closest, he told her that he was part of the traffic control based here in Berlin and he had just come off duty and was back at 6am.

"How do you manage on so little sleep?"

"We just do, we catch up when we have a few days off together."

It was quite late before Annabel had a chance to speak to Martina the stewardess who had invited her and the noise level had dropped so that she could hear what was being said. Martina explained that she had been flying for several years and really enjoyed her job and now that she had started to go out with an officer from the army base, she was enjoying her time in Berlin.

"Have you met many other officers and their wives, I was staying with an officer and his wife Lily on my last visit here to Berlin, do you know her?"

"Not really, I have heard that she and her husband are getting a divorce and she has returned to England. I also heard a rumour that she had been investigated for dealing drugs on the base, but I don't know if that is true."

Oh my God, thought Annabel, the parcel she gave me to take back could have been drugs, what if I had been stopped at customs?

Despite this information Annabel had an entertaining evening and it was very late when she at last got back to her hotel room. I wonder how the flight crew manage to party each night and still appear to be fresh the next morning ready to work. Berlin was turning out to be an amazing job and she was so pleased to have been asked to produce the Berlin Tattoo finale.

The rest of the rehearsals had gone well, and the dress rehearsal was spectacular to watch, where 500 men each holding two lit touches, finished with making a pattern of a thistle in the arena.

The first performance the next day was very well received and had tremendous applause from the audience and been congratulated by the Senior Officers for a job well done.

She went back-stage to thank the men for working so hard and apologised for giving them such a hard time, and told them that if any of them when they finished in the army wanted to contact her as she would take them on as dancers, which was received with much laughter.

Chapter Twenty-three
Trip to the Isle of Wight

Poppy had called to say that the course was good but very hard work as she had to produce five essays of 5000 thousand words each and had to do 420 hours of teaching over the length of the year. She had been out to work a few days at a nursery in 'nappy valley' in Battersea.

"Mum, the girls that I was working with there are not very friendly and gave me all the menial jobs to do and when we have a break in the staff room, they do not talk to me or offer to make me a cup of tea, although they made them for their friends."

"Poppy it is always the same when you go into a new work environment, you just have to try and win them over. Whatever happens just listen to the manager and do the work that is assigned to you to the best of your ability. Just remember that this work is only temporary just to give you the taste of what it is like to work at a Montessori nursery, your friends on the course you have told me are friendly and nice with you."

The Montessori School in London had a very good reputation and attracted students from all round the world and most came from affluent families as the course was very expensive. Poppy had, in the last month, torn a ligament in her knee and was in plaster which didn't help as the Montessori School where she was studying was on the top floor.

"How are you managing to get to class?"

"On my bottom one step at a time — but the girls who are on my course are very nice and at lunch go out and buy me a sandwich, so I don't have to climb the stairs too many times. And at the end of the day they help me into a taxi, and Gemma is being helpful when I get home and even cooks for me, which is a first! Mum, did you know that Gemma wants to leave Arts Educational school and go over to Spain and work at nightclubs doing promotional work?"

Annabel was surprised to hear this as Gemma had not spoken to her or David about leaving school. She had told her that she had been signed off from the mental health specialist but still refused to elaborate on the reason she had taken sleeping pills. Annabel had been advised not to keep asking as it was felt that Gemma would speak to her mother when she was ready.

Annabel was at home this weekend as David was on leave at last and all the children would be there too so she could speak to Gemma then about her new plans. What was worrying was that David had told her he was planning a day out on the boat over to the Isle of Wight and had asked several officers to join them, one of which was Oliver and his wife.

Saturday was bright and sunny, and David had left early with the boys to get the boat ready and Gemma and Poppy were going to help prepare lunch for them all.

"Gemma, I hear that you are thinking about leaving Arts and going away with Lucy to work in Spain."

"Mum, I am not enjoying the course at Arts and I don't really feel that I will get anywhere when I leave. You know I want to come and work with you in the agency so thought I would take a few months off if you and Dad agree. Please don't say no. I spoke to Dad this morning before he left, and he said that we would sit down this evening and discuss it. Lucy has got it all worked out and has received confirmation that we can work for the nightclubs handing out pamphlets on the beach during the day and in the evening, we can do some bar work. Lucy has also arranged with her parents that we can live in a friend's apartment in Marbella which is free for a few months."

Annabel was concerned that if she refused her permission Gemma might go anyway and she preferred to know all about their plans and exactly what work she would be involved in and importantly where they would be living. It seemed an age ago since she was a teenager and wondered if she had asked her mother if she could go away to Spain what the answer would have been. She was sure that it would have been a resounding 'No Way.'

Annabel had other things to think about this morning as Oliver was joining the family for the day which could be very uncomfortable for them both so she must not spend too much time speaking to him and be very careful not to look at him. She had only met his wife the one time at the ball and did not know how they would get on.

Annabel and the girls arrived at Gosport Marina with all the food for lunch and David had restocked the boat with plenty of cold drinks, wine and beer. The boys came down the jetty to help carry everything to the boat. David's friends had not arrived yet, so they had time to get everything ready.

"Ahoy there, can we board?" said a voice from the jetty and when Annabel looked everyone had arrived. Derek and Rosalind, Peter and Bianca and Oliver and Jamie.

"Welcome, aboard!" Everyone had brought a bottle and

some goodies to eat and they came onboard and were shown where to leave their bags. The women went to change into swimsuits and the men helped to untie the boat and set sail to the island. Annabel made coffee for everyone and when she handed a cup to Oliver their fingers touched which sent a charge through her body, and her breath caught in her throat. How was she going to get through this day with Oliver so close but out of bounds?

The men stayed with David and the women went on the bow of the boat to sit in the sun on the trip while the children amused themselves sitting on the deck.

Annabel had met Rosalind and Bianca before, and both were nice women. They had families and worked part-time so had much to chat about. Jamie, Oliver's wife did not work but volunteered at several charities.

"I understand that you are involved in a few charities. What do you do for them?" she asked.

"Well, mostly it is fundraising and putting on events which is very interesting. I understand that you recently put on a show for the Variety Club. Perhaps we could speak to you about doing the same for us?"

"Well, I would love to help but I can only organise one a year as it takes so much time and also getting the models to agree takes some persuading, but let me know when you have some idea of a date and I will see if I can be of help. Whatever, even if I cannot put on a show I maybe can help with some prizes for a tombola."

Jamie was very hard work as she only wanted to talk about the charity work she did. At last they arrived on the island and tied up at Cowes Marina and Annabel and the women went inside to prepare lunch while David organised the drinks.

It was so nice to be sitting in the sun, food always tasted better when eaten outside. Annabel couldn't help but sneak a glance at Oliver and saw that he was looking at her. Their eyes locked and images of them when they had last been together came into her mind, which made her feel hot, so she had to look away. She stood up to gather some plates and empty glasses inside to wash up and when she looked Oliver had followed her inside the cabin carrying some glasses.

"I don't think that this is a good idea, I do not want to cause you or your wife any trouble."

Oliver's hand touched Annabel' s fingers.

"Just to be near you is good for me, even better when I can touch you."

They looked at each other, smiling, so close was agony but better than being apart thought Annabel.

"Just imagine what I could do for you if we were alone," said Annabel and with that she put her hand on his crouch which was hidden from view, and gently squeezed him. She could feel him harden under her fingers.

With a grown Oliver moved quickly away to the cabin at the back.

The rest of the trip went by without any incident and by the time they got back to Gosport they were all tired but the men helped David wash the boat down and lock up.

'Thanks for a wonderful day they all said as they shook David's hand and gave Annabel a cuddle. Oliver leaned over and kissed her on the forehead as he gave her hand a squeeze.

Lovely day, lovely Oliver thought Annabel as she drove the children back home.

Chapter Twenty-Four
Lawn Tennis Association Fashion Show

The new office was up and running in Manchester Street, the two rooms had been knocked through and it made a much lighter place to work. Freddie was happy and seemed to be in his element, inviting the models and dancers to come in to see him, and had organised cakes and coffee for everyone. Annabel had to laugh as when she called in to the new office it was filled with male models. Freddie seemed to have quite a following!

Even more exciting was the lease which she had signed on the flat in Baker Street which was amazing. It was on the top floor, which was a pain. Why was she not able to find anything on the ground or first floor?

On opening the front door there was a small hall, with a cupboard for storage, a very large bedroom, bathroom next door and at the front of the building was the lounge which was enormous with two large floor to ceiling windows and a kitchen just off this room; large enough for a sink, cupboards, washing machine, a table, six chairs and a very pretty dresser.

She had the apartment redecorated and laid down new carpet; not expensive but durable and looked nice. She had ordered some curtains for the lounge which were her one big extravagance as they hung from the ceiling and pooled on the floor with layers of material. The bedroom had just muslin curtains and the bathroom and kitchen the same.

She had bought two new sofas which converted into beds in case she had anyone to stay but managed to use other items from the flat in the Kings Road. She had invested in a new bed and cupboard for the bedroom and some pretty linen, she also had a beautiful desk from home that David did not use anymore and it looked good in the lounge as it filled a space in the large room as she couldn't spend too much money on a flat that she was only using a few days a week so wanted to watch the pennies.

The agency has been asked to perform a fashion show for the Lawn Tennis Association for the centenary of the club. Many of the tennis stars would be attending such as Virginia Wade and Fred Perry and Her Majesty the Queen and Prince Philip which was a great honour for the agency.

She had met up with Charlie and Lindy to talk through the requirements and to select the dancers that they would use. She only wanted the very best dancers that were on the books. They arranged to meet up in London to visit the headquarters of the club in Wimbledon where the exhibition and show was to be held. Annabel also promised Charlie that before they looked at the venue, she would organise for her to visit the clothing manufactures whose merchandise they would be using. She had also been promised a selection of merchandise from 100 years ago to show what had been worn at that time; if it was not suitable, she had promised the organisers that she could have made a good example of what had been worn and would get approval before making which they were happy with.

Lindy and Annabel had stayed at the London flat so they

could arrive early for the dress rehearsal. They were well prepared, as rehearsals and fittings had gone well.

There was a hive of activity in the room they would be performing in with many TV crews also setting up. The stage and lighting rig were in place and the dressing room was organised with rails, tables and mirrors for the dancers. The merchandise arrived and Charlie took delivery and went with the backstage staff to organise the room while Lindy did a run with the music. As soon as the dressing room was ready, they did a dress run with the sound and lighting man to make sure all the cues he had been given were OK.

Lunch was served for all the staff working in the room and when they had finished were asked to clear the room as the security were going to come in with dogs to check that all was safe.

The Queen and Prince Philip arrived and were shown into the exhibition area to meet some of the tennis stars and after they had spent some time speaking with various members of the association were shown into the room where the show was being performed.

They sat in the front row and Annabel could see from her vantage point by the sound and lighting that they smiled the whole way through the performance.

After the show the dancers, Charlie, Lindy and Annabel were asked to line up at the side of the stage where the Queen and Prince Philip passed by and thanked everyone for a very enjoyable show.

Newspaper photographers asked some of the dancers to step on the stage so photos could be taken for the next day newspapers so it was quite late when they could get away. As she had driven up, Annabel took Lindy with her in the car.

Charlie had her own transport so did not need a lift.

On the way back to Portsmouth Annabel asked Lindy how she was.

"I have left my husband we have been together for many years, but it is just not working. I don't love him; in fact, I have been having an affair for the past year and we have decided to move in together. I am glad that we have been able to speak about this as there is something, I want to tell you — I am pregnant."

"Well, if that is something you are happy about many congratulations. When is the baby due?"

"Not for another six months and I can still work until the last month and I want to be able to come back and work again with you, my mother said that she will look after the baby for me. Do you think that will be possible? I love working for the agency and would hate to leave and quite honestly I need the money."

"Lindy I don't want you to leave and I will try and look for someone that can choreograph for me in your absence, perhaps one of the dancers that used to work for us but has now left might be willing to step in. Leave it with me and let me have a talk with Freddie; he knows what all the dancers are doing so perhaps he can recommend someone."

That was quite a surprise as she had no idea that Lindy was pregnant, she did not show yet and was fit and healthy so hopefully there would not be any problems. Something else for Annabel to think about, she really liked Lindy and had forgiven her for the unpleasantness that had occurred at the Variety Club so hoped she could find someone that could step in for a few months.

Gemma had spent the evening after the boat trip talking

with Annabel and David and told them how she did not feel she was gaining anything by staying at Arts Educational and wanted to take off for a spell but said she would call home every few days. Lucy's parents were also going to keep an eye on them and had already arranged a holiday in Marbella to see them during the time they would be working there.

Reluctantly Annabel and David had agreed but told Gemma that two months was the limit she could just 'bum around' and then she had to come home, and if there was a place available, she could work at the agency.

So, it was arranged and perhaps a new era was about to start for Gemma and she would grow up and take on some responsibility for herself. The other children had all settled down and were working hard, so now it was Gemma's turn.

Chapter Twenty-Five
Lunch and Dessert

Annabel invited Oliver up to London for lunch and to show him her new apartment. She had not seen him since the boat trip, as they had both been busy and had only spoken on the phone.

Oliver said that he wanted to take her out for lunch first, so there was no need for her to cook and they had arranged to meet the following day at a restaurant in Baker Street which was close to the apartment.

She spent the morning in the office with Freddie and had told him about Lindy being pregnant and said he thought he knew a dancer who had started to choreograph for music videos. He said he would talk to him about the possibility of stepping in for a few months and if they got really busy taking on some more shows for them.

Annabel went back to the apartment before going to the restaurant as she had a surprise she wanted to organise for Oliver. As she left, she put on her new raincoat which was of a very light material and belted at the waist. She arrived early at the restaurant and was asked if she wanted to leave her coat, but she declined and was shown to the table that Oliver had booked. She ordered some mineral water while she was waiting and was studying the menu when Oliver walked in and sat down at the table.

A big smile crossed Annabel's face as Oliver took her hand in his as he sat down.

"Hello beautiful lady, you look nice. Is that new? But now that I have seen it why you don't you take it off as you must be hot wearing it."

"I am glad that you like it, but I am really very cool as I am not wearing anything underneath. This is especially for you. Why don't you take off your shoes and put your foot on my leg and you will be able to feel me?"

Oliver slipped off his shoes and put one of his feet on Annabel's leg, she could feel his foot travelling up until it came to the top of her leg so she manoeuvred herself a little closer to the table so his foot was just on the tip of her vagina.

Oliver leaned on the table and stroked Annabel's hand while looking into her eyes.

"How am I going to concentrate on my lunch if I can feel you getting wet?"

"Well we must enjoy what we are eating but think of me as your dessert, and perhaps you can eat me later."

They studied the menus for a while and gave their orders to the waiter who was hovering near by, Oliver ordered a bottle of wine which was served quickly. The wine was a favourite of theirs and when poured drunk slowly from the glass.

"I thought that you looked gorgeous in your swimsuit you wore on the boat, but I must say that I prefer you wearing nothing at all. I like to look at you just standing in front of me without any clothes, your skin is so perfect and when I touch you it feels wonderful. You are silky smooth to touch and I can feel when I give you pleasure a heat raises through your body making you feel warm."

Annabel was also finding it difficult to concentrate on

what she was eating as all she wanted was to be close to Oliver and put her arms around him and feel him getting hard.

They finished quickly and Oliver asked for the bill, and when it came just threw some notes on the table such was the desire of the both of them to leave.

They walked back to the apartment. Annabel opened the front door of the building and they run up the stairs to the door of her apartment, on opening they could not wait, she banged the door closed and ripped off her coat. She stood slightly away from Oliver.

"Is this how you like me to be?" she asked.

Oliver threw off his clothes and without moving from the hall they closed the gap between them and lay on the floor. Oliver moved on top of her and without waiting pushed hard into her with his penis which was hard and throbbing and came in a rush grunting loudly.

"Oh, Annabel I am so sorry that I didn't wait for you, but I have been watching you during lunch and when I felt you getting wet it was all I could do to contain myself. Give me a short while and I promise that I will pleasure you all afternoon like you have never been pleasured before."

"Oh Oliver, it was exciting for me to see how much you wanted me. We have all afternoon to play. Come let me show you around but do you want a bath first?"

"No, just a towel will do for the moment. Lead on."

Annabel took Oliver first into the lounge and he admired the fabulous curtains and loved the way she had furnished the room, she then showed him the pretty kitchen and on to the bathroom and finally the bedroom.

"I would like to think of you lying in bed here when I am not with you."

Oliver moved Annabel onto the bed and put a pillow under her bottom and started to use his tongue softly round her clitoris licking her and breathing lightly on her until he could feel her start to get wet and her muscles tensing and her back arch.

He pushed his tongue into her vagina licking and sucking and then using his lips to kiss her with gentle kisses. He then moved away, "does that feel good?"

"Yes, please don't stop. I want to feel your tongue inside me again."

He moved his face closer to her and started to increase the pressure, rolling his nose up and down and side to side and then put his tongue inside thrusting it hard with quick movements and he could feel Annabel approach orgasm as she lifted her body up to meet his face. He put his fingers inside as she started to climax and came with a loud roar.

They lay on the bed holding hands while their breath slowly returned to normal.

"Oliver you did pleasure me, it was worth waiting for."

They spent the afternoon just sitting, kissing and listening to music until it was time for Oliver to go.

The apartment seemed so quiet that evening as Annabel sat thinking about the fabulous afternoon, they had spent together. She missed him every moment that they were not together, but in a way, it made it more enjoyable when they next met.

Chapter Twenty-Six
Filming on the Solent

While David had been home on leave, he had been asked by a friend if he was interested in hiring his boat out for about seven days, as a film company was filming in the Solent, a film based on the life of Aristotle Onassis, the Greek shipping magnate. Anthony Quinn was staring in the film and he had stipulated that he wanted a private boat to ferry him each day to and from the tanker that was moored in the Solent and was being used for the filming.

David was very excited about this and was happy to use his boat as a private taxi for Anthony Quinn. He had also been asked if he could organise the catering on board for the actors and crew during the week's filming and had recommended a good friend of theirs, Edna, who had done a lot of private catering.

David and Edna went down to the Camber to meet up with the location organiser early the next morning and was met by a young man who talked nineteen to the dozen and just fired out instructions at them.

"David you must be at the Camber each morning at 7 a.m. to take Mr Quinn and his guests out to the tanker then tie up alongside and wait until he needs to be bought back. At the end of the week you will need to report to the accounts office we have set up in the Queens Hotel in Southsea so you can be paid. And Edna you will need to cater for at least 120 people a day, so if you can bring the food here the day before we start shooting that will be ideal. I assume that you have your own catering trucks to transport the food and can organise fresh produce to be delivered each day when needed. I will arrange a boat to meet you to take the food on board."

Edna was just nodding and saying yes to everything that was being asked of her until the location manager tore out a blank cheque from a book and gave it to her.

"If you could keep all the receipts from your shopping and just write out the cheque to cover this, do you know how many staff you need to bring with you?"

"No, not yet. I need to work it all out, but I will call you with the number and also the cost of cooking and staff first thing tomorrow."

The man gave Edna his cell number and without a goodbye just walked away.

Annabel had also been asked to provide extras both on the tanker and in a studio outside London where they were filming some scenes which were supposed to be inside Onassis's private plane. They wanted three girls who must be very beautiful to act as stewardess.

David came home each night full of stories about the day's filming. He and his friend Derek who was crewing for him met with Anthony Quinn each morning who was always accompanied by several beautiful woman and took them over to the tanker where he tied up alongside until he was needed to return them to shore. He was also asked to motor around the tanker to keep any small boats away, so they were not getting too close while they were filming. When he had an opportunity, he would go on board to say hello to Edna who was always busy cooking the three meals a day required. She told him that the day before when there was a lull in the afternoon while they were setting up for the next scene, she had played cards with some of the kitchen staff and the director of the film had joined them and she won pots of money so treated them all to drinks that evening.

Anthony Quinn loved being on the boat and asked David if he could steer it across the Solent which he did most mornings.

At the end of the week's filming David duly arrived at the office which had been set up in the Queens Hotel and was given a large cheque for the use of his boat.

"Annabel, this means we can have a fabulous holiday with the children, where would you like to go?"

After much discussion with the kids it was decided that they would take a holiday in Malta which was where they had spent their honeymoon. Laying in the sun for two weeks with nothing much to do sounded like bliss to Annabel. She remembered during the 60s on honeymoon she had gone out shopping with David in Valetta, the main town in Malta, and was wearing a pair of shorts but was stopped by the police and told she was wearing inappropriate clothing and would she please go back to the hotel to change so her legs were covered. How times had changed!

Freddie had contacted the choreographer, Alan, he knew and had arranged for him to come into the office so he could meet Annabel and discuss how he might be able to help.

Annabel remembered using Alan in some of her shows and he was a good dancer and had also helped with rehearsals. He was married to a girl from Portsmouth and she had joined the agency so if it worked out it could be a good fit.

Before she went on holiday Annabel wanted to make sure that all loose ends were tied up and all the dancers booked for the forthcoming shows, so she and Freddie made lists of what needed to be done. The summer months were not usually busy so she did not expect that there would be any problems and if unexpected work came in Freddie could always call on a friend of his who sometimes worked in the office at busy times.

Gemma was due back from her time in Spain the next weekend and on the phone calls Annabel had received seemed to have really enjoyed her time working at a nightclub. The work that they had been promised had not materialised so the two girls had taken themselves off to the Sinatra Bar in the 'Pueto Banus' marina to have a drink and discuss what to do next as they had been told that if they didn't work, they must come home. While they were sitting in the bar with all the beautiful people, they had seen a man putting up a notice stating that help was wanted for a new nightclub which was soon to be opened by a British racing driver in Marbella.

"Mum, it was so funny, as soon as the man left Lucy and I took the notice down and then spent the rest of the day following him so he didn't see us, and every notice he put up we took down and threw away, so when the day of the interview arrived Lucy and I were the only girls who turned up, and guess what- we got the job."

The girls had spent the last few months doing all the jobs that were needed, serving behind the bar, being a DJ and even at times being a bouncer at the door. They had over time recruited extra staff as the place was heaving and was the most popular nightclub in the area. But now was the time for them to come home and after the holiday Gemma would go back to live with Poppy and start working at the agency.

143

Chapter Twenty-Seven
Time to Say Goodbye

The autumn seemed to fly by, and Annabel was pleased that Gemma had joined the agency as they really needed two people in the office as there was so much work coming in.

She fitted in well and it seemed that she had at last found something that she loved to do and had handled many jobs herself; speaking to the clients, booking the models and when necessary going out to make sure that the job was going well. She had also interviewed new models and promotional staff, so she had her own list to choose from.

Annabel had met up with Oliver many times both at home just meeting up for a drink or lunch in London when he had the time. She had received a phone call from him just before the Christmas break to say that he had some news to tell her but wanted to meet as he didn't want to tell her on the phone, so they arranged to meet in the pub in the country they both knew. It sounded rather worrying but she didn't want to speculate too much, or it would drive her mad thinking of all the different scenarios the news could be.

She arrived at the pub and it was pouring with rain, so she hurried inside and found Oliver sitting by an open log fire. He did not look very happy as she sat down next to him.

"Oliver, what is the matter? You look like you have the world's troubles on your shoulders."

"Annabel this has been in the pipeline for a few months now and I didn't want to tell you about it in case it never happened. I have been offered a new posting overseas which means I must leave England for the next few years. It is a big promotion and if I turn it down, I will not be asked again, and my career would be at a standstill."

Annabel just looked at Oliver and felt that the floor had been taken from under her feet, she did not know what to say, and she was nervous that if she spoke, she would start to cry.

Oliver took her hand in his, "my darling I do not want to leave you and I thought that perhaps I could ask you to come with me, but I know that is not possible as you have your children and career to think about and it would be an impossible situation for both of us."

As Annabel started to speak, she could feel her tears start.

"When do you have to give your answer and when would you leave?"

"Not till after Christmas, so we still have some time left to be together. I am so sorry the time I have spent with you has been the best part of my life. Your enthusiasm, your love, your beautiful face, your lovely body mean so much to me I really do not know how I will tear myself away."

They sat holding hands and not speaking very much. What was there left to say? As Annabel left the pub she walked slowly back to her car and although it was raining hard, she did not seem to notice as the rain mixed in with her tears and she felt that she could hardly catch her breath.

They knew that it would be difficult to meet over the Christmas holidays as they both had family commitments but arranged to meet up early in the new year when they could spend some time together and to say goodbye which Annabel knew would be one of the hardest things she would ever have to do.

Christmas that year was difficult. It had both a sweet and sad feeling about it, having all the children home for the holidays would help as she would be involved with them. They always made a big deal of Christmas; inviting friends and family over and entertaining was fun but at the back of her mind was always the thought that she had to say goodbye to the most beautiful man she had ever met. He made her feel like a special person not just someone's other half, but someone of importance in his life. How was she going to let him go?

They met in London shortly after New Year at the restaurant in Baker street they had been to before.

"Do you remember the last time we were here?" said Annabel with a smile, "and what I was wearing?"

"Not very much if I remember correctly, so I didn't have too many clothes to take off."

They spent the time reminiscing about the happy times they had spent together, holding hands and locking eyes as if they couldn't get enough of each other.

"Shall we leave now? I want to hold you close to me and I can't do the things I want to do to do here in the restaurant."

They went back to the apartment, walking slowly as if they hurried the time would just go too quickly. On entering the apartment, they spent their time slowly undressing one another and Annabel could feel Oliver's eyes drinking her in as if he wanted to remember every part of her body, so there was nothing that he would forget.

They made their way to the bedroom and Oliver laid her gently on her back, caressing every part, from her face down to her toes. She could see him taking delight in exploring her body, her mind, and heart.

He started to kiss her face, her eyes, neck, breasts and spent time playing with her nipples slowly sucking them and then moved down so he could put his tongue inside while holding her arms above her head so that she couldn't move.

"Let me sit on top Oliver, that way I can feel all of you when you enter me."

They changed positions so that Oliver was laying on his back and Annabel began to work on him slowing kissing his body while she played with his balls. She then moved down so that she could take him in her mouth slowly moving her tongue round him until she could feel him harden.

She moved her face away and moved her body so that she was sitting on his cock and with a gentle movement pushed so that he was completely inside her.

"I love you Oliver, you are my soulmate my beloved," and with each movement she made she could feel him reach the organism they each wanted, and they came together in a blinding climax.

"I love you Annabel, my sweet, beloved girl."

They spent the rest of the afternoon just exploring each other bodies until it was time to leave.

They caught a train back to the south coast and sat quietly not talking very much just holding hands under his coat. Oliver was to get off a station before Annabel and as they neared the station Oliver learned over and without speaking just kissed her on her forehead.

She watched him get off the train and saw that he looked so unhappy, her own tears were flowing down her face, she couldn't stop them. As the train left the station, she saw that Oliver had not moved, and as the train gathered speed, she couldn't see him anymore. He had gone.

PART TWO

Chapter Twenty-Eight
A 21st Birthday Celebration

Gemma had been out with some promotional staff for a product launch and was approached by a man who asked if the agency were interested in producing a dancing fashion show for Lord Althorp's 21st birthday party to be held at the family's private home in Mayfair. He said that he had heard of the agency and knew of the work they did. He wanted to know how much the cost of a show lasting about 30 minutes would be.

Gemma thought that the that the request was not something that was genuine and gave a figure of £10,000 to include the complete production of the show using 10 dancers. She gave him the agency's card and asked if he would telephone in the next few days to confirm if the price was acceptable and to give details of the event.

She did not think that she would hear from him again and was surprised to receive a phone call early the next morning in the office.

"Good morning, am I speaking to Gemma? If you recollect, we spoke yesterday evening when I asked if you could help us with a show. I would like to confirm that we would like your agency to produce the show for us and will send you written confirmation of the date and address. Please will you confirm back to me the names of all the personnel that will be coming, together with their full details including a photo and a copy of their passport as there will be many of the young royal family attending and we need to check-up on everyone involved."

After he rang off, she telephoned Annabel who was at home that morning and told her of the bizarre conversation she had just had.

"Mum, I really do not know if this is genuine but as soon as I receive written confirmation, I think that we should check this out."

Annabel agreed and told Gemma that if she received written details, she would telephone the police.

Later that morning a courier delivered a letter and Gemma phoned through to Annabel who then spent the next hour checking the legitimacy of the contract. She was delighted to hear that all was well, in fact the officer she had spoken to at the police station said that he hoped that they enjoyed the evening.

What was even more surprising was to have a security company turn up with an envelope, which when opened contained £10,000 in cash.

All the dancers wanted to be included and the office was besieged by calls from them begging to be booked, even saying that they would work backstage as a dresser.

Selecting the most beautiful garments to be used was so easy as many of the companies that Annabel approached were more than willing to lend their merchandise, even offering outfits for Gemma and herself. Gemma was going to style the show as she had brought the job in and by that time had had much experience in selecting clothes for promotions and shows with great success. Charlie had taken a step back as her boutique had by this time closed and she wanted to pursue other ventures.

After the selection of the dancers was made and confirmed Freddie organised paperwork to be sent out to them requesting the documents needed for the evening and also informing them that before entering the house, they would all have to sign to say that nothing they saw or heard during the evening was to be discussed.

All the crew involved in the production arrived early in the morning at Spencer House, St James's which was a most beautiful house and had been restored to its original splendour. They were met at the door by security and Annabel handed over all the documents they had requested.

The merchandise arrived soon after and a busy morning with a dress run and organising the room to be used for clothes changes was done. They were very well looked after with a continuous supply of sandwiches and cold drinks sent to the room.

The show was to be performed later that evening about 10 p.m. after a live video link to the US had been made and Whitney Houston had sung *Happy Birthday*. No one could leave the building during the day, but the time went by very quickly with sneaky looks at some of the rooms on the ground floor when they had a break. That afternoon they were asked to leave the room that was being used as a dressing room so that the dogs could come in and the security men could do their checks.

At 8 p.m. they could hear the guests arriving, and much laughter and talking could be heard from the ballroom. In the background music was playing and they had heard that after the show there would be a disco for the guests. Supper was served in another room and after it was finished Annabel crept into the ballroom and stood at the back when a very pretty girl came in and sat down in front of her holding hands with her man and was giggling with him. It wasn't long before Annabelle realised that it was Princess Diana and Prince Charles.

The show was very well received and after each scene there was much applause from the audience until it was all over, and they took a final bow.

Lord Althorp came backstage after the show to say thank you and sent through bottles of Champagne and food for everyone.

It was well after midnight by the time all the merchandise had been packed away and the room tidied. The dancers, Gemma and the staff who had helped backstage had gone which just left Lindy and Annabel to collect their belongings and leave.

As she went to say goodnight one of the security men asked Annabel for the remaining papers that everyone had signed to be handed over.

"But I am sure that they were handed in when we arrived"

"No, not all of them, and I am sorry, but you cannot leave the premises until we have everything."

With that Lindy and Annabel unpacked everything until they found in the last packing case the file, by which time it was 3 a.m.

At last they had finished and as they left the building a few photographers from the newspapers were still hanging around hoping that they could catch a photo of some of the young royals.

"Annabel, how was the party? What did you see? Can you

tell us?"

"No comment," said Annabel with a laugh "I don't want to be taken to the Tower of London!"

Dawn was coming up as they arrived back in Portsmouth and Annabel dropped Lindy at home. What a great day and what stories she could tell.

Chapter Twenty-Nine
Ski Show

The agency had organised shows at The Ski Exhibition in London for the second year running and Annabel had heard that the organiser Austin had an offer from the Daily Mail to buy the show from him on a very good deal.

Austin was running around the exhibition like a headless chicken and trying to do everything himself and he was in a very bad mood when he caught up with Annabel during the run-up to the show opening

"Why can't you listen when I tell you that you cannot run a dress rehearsal with music when the BBC are trying to record?"

"I am sorry Austin, but you did not tell me, and I did not get a message that you wanted silence in the hall, or I would have waited until I got the all clear."

"Well you are a stupid girl; you should have known," and he stormed off back to his office

That was just too much for Annabel as she was very tired and Austin shouting at her was the last straw, so she crept beneath the stage where there was no one about and sat down and started to cry.

As she was sitting in the dark a very good-looking man came up to her and asked if everything was OK. She did not know who he was as had not seen him before.

"I am fine, please don't concern yourself, it is just me being stupid."

But the man did not want to take that as an answer. He wanted to know why she was crying and who had upset her, and after much persuasion she told him about Austin and the unfairness of his complaint. With that he walked out, and she did not see him again for the next hour.

While she was backstage with the dancers she was asked if she would please go to the organiser's office as the editor of The Daily Mail wanted to speak to her.

When she entered the office, she saw Austin with the man who she had spoken with.

"Annabel, I am sorry I should have introduced myself to you, I am David and for my sins I am editor of The Mail. I think Austin has something he wants to say to you."

A very sheepish and embarrassed Austin came up to Annabel put his arms around her and said that he was very sorry for shouting, but he was under a lot of strain, and would she forgive him?

Annabel was flabbergasted that the editor had taken the time to confront Austin and make him apologise; that was a first. After she had told Austin that she accepted his apology David took her arm.

"Come on Annabel, let me take you for a drink and you can tell me about your agency and what things you do."

They spent a very pleasant hour at the bar and Annabel told him that besides producing shows she could also bring in sponsorship and in fact she was in discussion with a leading ski wear store who would be interested in the exhibition for next year as they wanted the whole of the fashion show just to show their merchandise, and also were looking at the possibility of a stand at the exhibition.

David said that he was always interested in sponsorship deals and if he could help in anyway, she must let him know. In the meantime, he would get the new exhibition organiser to contact her so that they could start discussions.

The first day of the exhibition was amazing with crowds just pouring in non-stop, and all the stands were busy selling their merchandise. The organiser had a very large slope built in the middle of the hall on which three times a day a 'Fantasia' ski aerialist show was performed with all the leading ski aerialists from around the world. Just watching this show brought gasps from the audience and great cheers went up each time a jump was completed. Annabel had met the team who were performing, and Gemma had started to go out with one of them. They seemed like nice boys, but it was worrying as they seemed to take their life in their hands each time they performed.

Poppy, Barry and Simon had come to the show as they all loved to ski and thought the exhibition was great fun and Annabel had promised them all that they could have some new ski wear for their next trip out to the slopes.

She found time during the day to call in to the office and as she didn't want Freddie to feel left out, she had given him some passes to the exhibition for him to use and bring some of his friends.

In the middle of the week while she was standing in the VIP area watching the aerialist show she was approached by a man who introduced himself as the owner of the company who had supplied the rig for the show including both the slope and lighting. He was dressed in jeans and t-shirt and looked like one of the stagehands not the owner of the company.

"Hey, I have seen you here each day are you involved in the exhibition?"

"Just the fashion show, but I would love to have had the opportunity of producing the Fantasia, it looks like fun and there is so many things that you could do with the show not just jumps. My name is Annabel by the way"

"Hello, I am Julian, pleased to meet you. Would you like to have a bird's eye view of the next performance? I can take you up on the lighting rig."

Annabel looked up to the lighting rig which seemed to be suspended at the top of the hall and wondered whether she was brave enough to watch the show from so high up. But why not give it a go?

"OK Julian but you will have to take very good care of me, I have never climbed so high up."

They arranged to meet before the next show and Annabel waited by the slope ready to take the climb, her heart was beating so fast as this was not something she had ever done before.

Julian arrived and showed Annabel how to climb the steel ladder up to the rig and assured her that he would be right behind her. Slowly she put one foot on the first step and holding on very tightly she climbed to the top where there was a platform. As soon as both her feet were on the platform, she opened her eyes which had been closed while she was climbed; the view was amazing and as long as she kept still, she was sure that she would be OK. Going down was another problem but one she would come to at the end of the show.

It was another world up here thought Annabel and watching the aerialists perform, they seemed like birds as they took off from the ramp and flew through the air to land perfectly on the air bag.

"Come on love we should go down now."

Annabel looked down and froze, she just could not move, she must have gone very pale as Julian took hold of her and said quietly, "Look Annabel we have to climb down but I will go in front of you and hold you close to me, just close your eyes and when I tell you just take a step at a time, backwards."

Annabel was shaking so much as she did as Julian told her and with her eyes closed managed to descend to the ground.

"It's Ok Annabel, you are safe now you can open your eyes," said Julian with his arms still round her. She felt so stupid. What on earth had possessed her to make the climb in the first place?

"I think what you need now is a stiff drink. Give me half an hour and I will take you out so I can buy you that drink and if you have the time perhaps, we can have something to eat."

They found a small restaurant close to Olympia and as it was early was quite empty; she was pleased as she did not want to see anyone from the exhibition just at the moment.

"I am sorry Julian that was so silly of me to have caused such a fuss, I am just not very good with heights, but I thought that I would be OK, please forgive me."

"Nothing to forgive, here I am sitting with a damsel I have just rescued, having a very pleasant evening."

When Annabel looked, she could see that Julian was a very attractive young man who seemed to be enjoying her company, so she began to relax and enjoy her time with him. It wasn't often that a man much younger wanted to spend time with her; it was very flattering — who was she to say no.

Two bottles of wine later and a really good meal Annabel was not feeling any pain and when Julian suggested they go to his hotel for a nightcap she did not say no.

As they entered his hotel room, they quickly threw off their clothes, their hands were all over each other's bodies, but Annabel did manage to ask that he had some protection. He went to the bathroom and brought back a condom.

"Give it to me, I will put it on for you," with that she took the wrapper and started to tear it open while kissing him all the way down his body until she came to his cock which she took in her mouth and sucked slowly until he was wet and then slowly put it over him.

Julian turned Annabel onto her back so that he could kiss her, starting with her lips and then moving slowly down to her breasts, he took her nipples into his mouth and started to suck on them until they became hard whilst putting his fingers inside her and stroking her.

Hands, lips, fingers were all over each other probing touching until Julian sat astride her and put his engorged cock inside and with quick thrusts he came.

"Now for your turn," he said as he went down on her putting his tongue inside her and rolling it round and making small bites with his teeth, Annabel could feel the heat slowly raise up her body and as her back arched she reached her climax and came.

Annabel left with no promises to call or to meet up again, just a very pleasant evening with a very nice and exciting young man.

Chapter Thirty
Paris

Gemma was going out most evenings to either parties or nightclubs and she had met a chamming French man who had told her that he worked for Thierry Roussel, the husband of Christina Onassis and he had invited her and a friend to the 40th birthday party of Christina to be held in France at their chateau.

"Mum, would you like to come with me? The party is in two weeks' time and they will send us tickets for the flights and put us up at the chateau for three nights."

"Are you sure that you want to take me? Would you not prefer to ask Lucy?"

"No, I really would like you to come with me, it would be such fun. I understand that they have invited many other model agencies from around the world and it is a chance for us to dress up and meet other agents. We both would need new evening dresses so we could go shopping, what do you think?"

Annabel had to laugh, was this a ploy to get her to buy Gemma a new outfit? Well, why not? She could do with a few days away in France and with all expenses paid it sounded like an opportunity she could not miss.

Gemma had arranged with Henri that they would like to stay an extra night after the party in Paris at their own expense so that they could take the opportunity of visiting a couple of agents that they had corresponded with who had booked several models to work for their clients in Paris.

The tickets for the flights had been sent to Gemma with instructions to telephone when they landed so that a car and driver could meet them and drive them straight to the chateau in the Loire Valley.

On arrival in Paris after they had collected their luggage Annabel asked Gemma to telephone through to the company that was collecting them. Gemma looked through her handbag but could not find the piece of paper where she had written the number on.

"Don't worry Mum I will phone Lucy at the flat I am sure that she hasn't left for work yet." After countless calls which all went through to a voice message Gemma and Annabel realised that they were stuck at the airport until Lucy could go home and find the note where the contact details were. Poppy who lived with them had gone away for a long weekend and was not going to be able to help.

Sitting at Orly airport for most of the day was not what they had both thought they would be doing that day but until Lucy could retrieve the number they were stranded.

"Come on Gemma this is stupid we better take a taxi into Paris and book ourselves into a hotel for the night and when Lucy eventually arrives home, we will be able to call for our lift."

It was very late that evening after booking into the hotel that Gemma was able to contact Lucy and at last the details were found. Gemma made a call and it was arranged that a car and driver would collect them the following afternoon.

Having to spend the day in Paris sitting on the Champs Elysees was not the hardest thing in the world and Annabel

163

had told Gemma that she had forgiven her as this was an opportunity of spending time together in the most wonderful city. They arrived back to the hotel and arranged to book in for their last night in Paris before they flew home. Annabel left her credit card details with reception to pay for that night and the booking on Monday.

They were collected by a limousine and driver in full livery and driven to the chateau early evening and felt very grand sitting in the back of the car.

On arrival the were astounded by the magnificence of the home they would be staying at for the next few days. The whole of the front of the chateau was ablaze with light and the long drive up to the grand front door was lit by flaming torches.

As they got out of the car the doors were opened by a butler and a young liveried man to collect their cases. They were shown up to their room which was enormous, probably as large as the whole of Gemma's flat with two double beds, beautiful carved wardrobes, a seating area with several sofas and a writing desk near the windows which looked out onto the grounds. There was a bathroom with a claw-foot bath with gold taps and so many soft white towels it was impossible to count.

The party was that evening, so they dressed in their new outfits and went downstairs to meet the other guests. Henri greeted them at the bottom of the stairs.

"My dear, what an unfortunate start to your stay with us, but do not worry I will try and make you forget, and you will both have a good time."

He took their arms and showed the into the room where the party was held and showed them to their seats and introduced them to the other guests at the table.

The party was in full swing by then and Annabel apologised for being late. The meal was superb, and the very best wines were being served. Christina came around to say hello and said that she hoped they would enjoy their stay. After the meal an enormous cake was wheeled in on a trolley on top of which sat a bird cage with two doves which were let out when everyone sang *Happy Birthday*.

Later that evening there was a cabaret with some of the cast from the Folies Bergère who had been flown in especially from Paris and it was very late when the party disbanded and all the guests went up to their rooms to bed.

The next morning Annabel and Gemma went down to the breakfast room and discussed what was available for them to amuse themselves with that morning.

"You can take either a sailboat or speed boat out on the lake. Horses are available for you to ride at the stables, or several quad bikes are at your disposal. After lunch is served at 1pm we are invited to the home of Thierry Roussel's father where you can swim or just laze around."

What a choice, Annabel wanted to walk around the magnificent estate while Gemma said that she always wanted to ride a quad bike and was taken to the area where they were kept.

Later that morning Gemma arrived back looking a little worse for wear.

"Mum, it was great fun but unfortunately I drove the bike into a ditch and had to climb out that is why I am covered in mud. I found a game keeper and reported the accident and wanted to walk back to show him where the quad bike was but he said not to worry they would find it sometime and he arranged for me to be brought back."

After lunch the guests were taken to Thierry Roussel's father's home and shown into the indoor swimming pool area. The solarium walls were covered with stuffed animals that his father had shot, which was not something that Annabel wanted to see. There seemed to be many more guests here and most looked like front-page models and were just laying around the pool. The guests who did not have swimwear were shown a cupboard full of the most exotic swimwear all still in their original packaging and in every size, you could think of.

A supper was laid on back at the chateau for the guests that were staying over that night. Thierry and Christina had already left by helicopter back to Paris.

The next morning Annabel and Gemma were driven back to Paris to spend the day visiting the model agents they had come to see. They had a light meal in a restaurant close to the hotel they were staying at and the next morning when they went to check out and pay, they were told that the bill had already been settled.

It was the most amazing experience they both had ever had and had been treated so well and made so welcome it was hard to know how to say thank you.

On returning home the next day Annabel sent a letter thanking Henri for including them in the birthday celebrations and asking him to please contact them when he was next in London so that they could take him out to lunch.

A few days later a message was left on the home answering phone.

"It was my pleasure it was so nice to see such beautiful ladies and we would like to invite you to South Africa next month for a safari, and in the meantime, I send you kisses."

This message did not go down well with David when he heard it and he refused to allow Annabel to go.

Chapter Thirty-One
Family Time

Annabel was staying at home for the next few days as David had some leave owing to him and they wanted to spend the time with the children. Annabel also felt that she needed some quiet time with David as they had not really spoken very much to each other over the last few months and things had been very strained between them. She did not know what the matter was as David was certainly not his usual happy self and perhaps if they could talk without any interruptions from the children, she might have the opportunity of asking him if anything was troubling him.

She made a nice meal for them both with his favourite wine and brought up the subject while they were sitting after eating in the lounge.

"David, I feel something is wrong and if you do not tell me I can't help."

"Nothing is wrong I just feel like a spare part when I am at home, you seem to have everything sorted and there is nothing left for me to do."

"David, that's so unfair. You're away so much of the time I have to sort things out with the children and the house so that when you come home you don't have to worry about any details. Maybe you should request a shore-based position so that you can be at home. You've been stationed away for all of our married life do you not think that we should spend more time together now."

"I love my job and do not want to be based here in Portsmouth, perhaps we could move to another country so that we can be together more of the time."

Annabel looked at David with amazement. What was he asking her to do? Give up her home? Leave the children? Give up her agency? And to what end? So that she could sit waiting for him in another country without her family and friends? Nothing would change except that she would be alone. That was not the answer. They both looked unhappy and perhaps something must change, but what? They would both have to make compromises to make things work.

They sat for the next few hours talking about the situation but no conclusions were reached that they could both agree on, so it was decided to have this conversation again after the weekend as it was not fair to either of them to leave things as they were.

Poppy came back from London full of stories about her time at the Montessori School and told her parents that she wanted to open a nursery in London when she had finished her course.

"There is a girl who I am very friendly with on the course and we have both decided that after spending some months working at nurseries to gain experience, we want to open a Montessori nursery together. We both feel passionate about children and the whole environment of nursery schools and her parents have a house in north London that is let out at the moment but in a year, they would be agreeable to let us run the nursery from there."

David and Annabel thought that Poppy had made a good

decision for her future and offered whatever help they could give her to succeed with the venture.

"You need to find out more about running a nursery school. Perhaps you can get advice from one of your tutors. It would be a good idea if you could find out if there is also a demand for nursery places in the area you are thinking of opening in; perhaps phone the local council and ask them."

Poppy was excited about the prospect of owning her own nursery and wanted to talk about the venture most of the weekend, but the other children were due home, so Annabel had to make sure that time was given to each of them.

One of the discussions she wanted to have was with Gemma to see if she was now willing to talk about the time she had taken sleeping pills as Annabel had had a rather disturbing conversation with one of her close friends, Patricia, who had confided in a rather nasty experience she had had with her doctor who was the same family doctor they were with.

Patricia had told her that on a visit to have a coil inserted by the doctor he had spent much time playing with her by putting his fingers inside for a lot longer than Patricia felt was necessary. He was doing this while standing close to the end of the bed she was laying on and looked very red in the face when he had finished. She had refused to go back to the surgery and had registered with another practice. Annabel wondered if this doctor had in any way abused Gemma as she was adamant that she did not want to see him again after she had been released from hospital. She had to handle this conversation very carefully as Gemma still might not want to talk about it.

Simon was coming back from university and bringing a friend with him for the weekend. The children's friends were always welcome, and Annabel was looking forward to meeting Simon's friend. Simon had told her the time his train was arriving, and Annabel was waiting to collect him at the station.

"Hi Mum, this is Ben," said Simon as he climbed into the car.

"Hi boys, glad to have you home Simon and welcome Ben, to Portsmouth."

Ben seemed like a nice young man, very well-dressed unlike her son who always looked such a mess. She remembered a call she had received from his last school on the Isle of Wight saying that could she please send Simon back after the holiday in a clean, tidy school uniform. She had taken Simon out and bought him a complete new set of clothes which he was wearing when she dropped him at the ferry but as he got out of the car, he fell and landed in a puddle. She had quickly driven away, let the school deal with it; she was paying enough!

Gemma arrived at home the same time as Annabel so at last the whole family was in one place. She found a pile of dirty clothes by the washing machine from all of the kids, what did they think she was running; a laundrette!

The fridge was raided by the hungry crowd and music was turned up to a very high level, but she loved it. Having the whole family together was the best.

After lunch Annabel had the chance to speak to Gemma on her own and told her about the incident that her friend had experienced with their family doctor.

"Gemma, it was very worrying to hear this and I need to ask if you had ever had the same thing happen to you?"

Gemma burst into tears which was all the confirmation that Annabel needed.

"Darling why did you not tell me this before when I could

have done something about it. The doctor died in the last month which was why we were talking about him. I would have confronted him and certainly reported him to the medical board, I feel so helpless now."

When Gemma had stopped crying, she explained that she had in fact tried to talk about it but every time she had started the conversation she just couldn't speak about this horrible man and what had happened to her.

"I am sorry Mum, but I felt so alone and did not have anyone to talk to so I thought if I took some sleeping pills it would take the pain away. I did speak about this to the mental health team and they really did help, but now it is so long ago I would prefer to forget about it and move on."

Annabel took Gemma in her arms and they stayed like that for a while until they could speak.

"My darling girl, please in future, if there is anything you want to talk about, I am here. I won't judge you I will just listen."

The rest of the weekend went well with much talking, laughter and fun, Barry had invited his latest girlfriend to join them, so it really was a full house.

After everyone had left Annabel thought that she and David should sit down and talk but he had seemed reluctant to take up the conversation and said that they would talk more on his next leave, which wasn't very satisfactory but she had to respect his wishes.

She had much to think about and felt rather drained with all that had gone on but she was so lucky in so many ways that she felt that perhaps someone was looking after her and that she only had the problems that she could cope with. No problems, only solutions she thought as she turned out the light.

Chapter Thirty-Two
Varity Club Spectacular

The agency was going well with much work coming in for both the models and dancers and the big productions as a central feature at the exhibitions was all that Annabel had hoped for.

"Hey Boss, do you want me to start on the booking of the dancers for the Variety Club show," said Freddie from behind a large pile of photos on his desk. They had been asked to produce a very large production fashion show based on the show in the West End *Chess* using the theme and the music. Tim Rice who had written the show had given his permission to use it and all the proceeds were going to disadvantaged children as before. The Chief Barker's wife was organising everything and it was a very big deal for the agency, with 30 models and dancers and a stage set being built especially for the event which was being held at The Grosvenor House Hotel in Park Lane, London.

"I think, Freddie, that we need to use our very best dancers and the tallest models we have on our books as the merchandise is all designer wear and the tall models would look stunning wearing these outfits."

They spent the next few hours looking through the files and selecting the cast that they wanted to use. They all had to be contacted to find out their availability as they all worked for several agents.

"Freddie you start on phoning around as I have an appointment in 20 minutes in Harley Street to see that eye specialist about my blocked tear ducts so will come straight back after."

Annabel hated spending time on herself, but her doctor had recommended that she see this specialist as her eyes were causing her some irritation as she had to keep wiping away the tears.

"I have an appointment with Mr. Shawn Rogers," said Annabel when she had arrived at the consulting rooms in Harley Street and was shown where to wait. It was not long before she was asked to follow the receptionist.

On opening the door, she saw that Mr. Rogers was intently looking at something on his computer, so she waited until he had finished. When he looked up, she was met with a charming smile and he stood up and came around his desk to shake her hand

"Hello, I am Shawn Rogers, please do take a seat and tell me what the problem is."

Mr. Rogers was an extremely attractive man of about 50 years old, dark black hair, greying at the temples, and his eyes crinkled up when he smiled which was often. What Annabel also noticed was that he was very well-dressed. What on earth was she thinking? She was here to ask him about her eyes not where he bought his suits.

"I have all your notes from your doctor, and I see that this problem has been going on for quite some time, tell me how it affects you."

Annabel explained that she was constantly wiping her eyes as the tears were running down her face which was not something she needed as she then had to repair her make-up, and as she was always on show in front of people. "It's become embarrassing."

"Are you a model?"

"No," laughed Annabel and then told him that she had a model agency and they spent the next half an hour talking about her work, which he seemed very interested in, and about the big show she had coming up for the Variety Club.

After he had examined her eyes, he told her that she needed to have the tear ducts in her eyes cleaned out which was a very simple procedure and if she would speak to his receptionist an appointment could be arranged.

He stood up when the consultation had finished and took her hand in his to say goodbye.

"It has been a real pleasure meeting you Annabel and thank you for telling me so much about your work, it sounds fascinating."

He opened the door to show her out. What a charming man thought Annabel as she made her way to the front desk to make the appointment.

On arriving back at the office, she found Freddie busy on the telephone and the other phones were ringing so she immediately set about helping. Gemma was out with a client, so it was just the two of them.

At last the hectic few hours was coming to an end and she and Freddie were able to take a breather and get a coffee. Most of the models and dancers had been contacted so they now had to wait to see who was available.

Before she left for the day, she had received a call from Mr. Rogers' secretary to say that the appointment had been changed and was now with another consultant for the following week. Annabel was sorry that she was not seeing Mr. Rogers again and was not sure why it had been changed so quickly, but perhaps an emergency had come in.

The next few weeks were busy as the music selection for *Chess* with Michelle had to be organised and she knew that it would take more than a few days as Michelle was very particular on which piece of music should go into which scene to complement the clothes. Alan, the choreographer she was using as Lindy was on maternity leave got on very well with Michelle so that helped. Gemma was selecting the merchandise and arranging for several exotic headdresses to be made to use in the swimwear scene.

On the day of the show they all arrived very early at The Grosvenor House Hotel to set up. The stage and lighting rig were still being finished so that they had to use another part of the ballroom to rehearse in.

Gemma was in the dressing room with Michelle organising the merchandise, rails, dressing tables and mirrors, and they had a makeup artist and two hair stylists to help.

It seemed to Annabel that with all the people in the ballroom it was more like a war zone than a dress rehearsal. The staff from the hotel were trying to dress the tables whilst members of the Variety Club were putting place cards on the tables as many of the show business people would be attending that evening. Beautiful flower arrangements were being brought in to put on the tables and cleaners were trying to clear away the mess.

The crew were still finishing the rig so Annabel went over to find out what time they could use the stage. She was told in one hour it would be available for her, so she went backstage to inform everyone that they could take a quick break and then be ready in an hour to start the dress run. She then went over to the sound deck and asked to use the microphone and announced that in one hour everyone must clear the stage and area in front as they were starting a dress run and please would everyone keep as quiet as possible while this was going on.

When the final dress rehearsal had been performed Annabel arranged for all her crew to have drinks and food delivered backstage and she at last had the opportunity of arranging her table that she had booked for her own friends and special clients as it was a way to say thank you to them. Unfortunately, David was away but had telephoned her earlier in the day to wish her much success.

Annabel did not have time to go back to the apartment to change but she had brought with her one of the evening, designer dresses to wear and after she had finished her own hair and makeup she went out into the ballroom. It all looked spectacular all the tables were dressed in white linen tablecloths and gleaming cutlery and glasses with flowers and candlesticks on each table. The stage was in darkness except for a small spotlight at the back of the set which had a table and two chairs and, on the table, sat a chess board which was illuminated.

The guests arrived and it was exciting to see so many famous faces and after dinner was finished the lights went down in the ballroom and the overture of the show started to play, the stage was lit up and the show began.

It was probably one of the best productions that Annabel had ever been involved in and she applauded with the audience when the show was finished. She was so proud of everyone that had taken part. Tim Rice went on Stage to thank everyone and said that if he had known how spectacular the show could be, he would have used Annie's Agency instead of spending so much money on his own production, which was received with much laughter.

After Annabel had gone backstage to thank everyone, she went to the bar to have a quiet five minutes and saw Shawn Rogers standing there on his own.

"This is a surprise, how nice to see you, I didn't know that you were attending Mr. Rogers."

"Shawn please, after you had told me about this show I telephoned and booked the last table available as it sounded like it would be a spectacular evening."

"Shawn, thank you for coming I am sure that the Variety Club has made a lot of money for their charity thanks to everyone that has supported this evening."

"I am sorry Annabel that I had to cancel your appointment with me, but I hope that the procedure went well."

"Yes, all is fine. I am sorry that an emergency came up so that I had to see another consultant."

Shawn spent a moment before he answered and then looked at Annabel as he spoke.

"No emergency, but I thought that it might be better if you saw someone else for your medical needs."

"My medical needs!" Annabel looked at him and then she thought that she understood. He was saying that he would like to see her, she did not know how to answer, so just took his hand and smiled.

" Another time perhaps," she said as she walked away

The next morning the office phones were ringing nonstop and flowers arrived from The Variety Club with a lovely note to say thank you, but the nicest surprise of all was an enormous bouquet of flowers which had a card which just had the name *Shawn* on it and a mobile phone number.

Chapter Thirty-Three
A New Friend

Annabel had started to work with major car companies and had been asked by the Ford Motor company to visit their head office in Brentwood in Essex as they wanted to discuss a roadshow tour and dealership shows for their new model coming out. She had arranged to meet the promotions executive, Carl.

"Annabel I would like you to quote for a three-month tour at all the major shopping centres which have an weekly footfall of about 500,000. We will need you to submit a detailed proposal of the stand, promotional staff and set build. I will send you the dimensions of the cars we want to exhibit so that you can make sure the access into the shopping centres is OK. Also, once that tour has finished, we then want to have special promotions evenings at a few of the dealerships, but we want those evenings to be more than just a look at the new car. What can you suggest?"

"Carl, you have seen our work before, and you know what we can do, I am sure that you want both the men and women to attend so, why not let us organise a fashion show with the car as the star. This would appeal to the man and his wife; the show would be exciting; about 20 minutes long with the commentary highlighting the benefits of your new Ford model. We can provide the complete production including the compere, and I promise it won't break the bank."

Carl was smiling as he looked through the portfolio Annabel had brought with her.

"Sounds good Annabel, I like the sound of the dealership evenings but a piece of advice, please don't write me a long proposal. I like your suggestions and as long as the price is right you will have a contract, so just one page with the proposal. I never read anything that goes on for too long."

Annabel thought that this was very good advice; keep the proposal short and to the point, she would remember this in all future meetings. She promised Carl that she would come back to him within the next two weeks with something he could take to the board.

This was something she had to work on herself as she needed to speak to all the shopping centres and get the data she needed so Freddie and Gemma would have to take care of business while she worked on it.

After about a week she had a good file of information so that the roadshow tour made sense in terms of location and venues and her next step would be to visit the centres to meet the management, book them up provisionally until Ford had confirmed and then the tour could be organised.

She had arranged for Carl to visit her at the office in Manchester Street so that she could talk him through both the selection of centres and costings for each one.

The day Carl visited the office was busy with models and Annabel introduced him to both Freddie and Gemma before taking him out for lunch so that they could talk in relative peace. He liked what she had given him and said that he would recommend both the roadshow tour and dealership evenings. They spent a pleasant hour talking about the industry and Carl told her that he had been working for Ford for many years before he was promoted to promotions executive and loved that side of the business.

Annabel arrived back at the office in a very happy mood as the roadshow tour was a very good piece of business to have.

"Hey Boss, did you hear that one of our models is going out with one of The Beatles, Beatles as in the pop group?" Freddie loved to pass on the gossip and he always seemed to be the first one to hear anything.

"Are you sure? The newspapers haven't printed this story yet, so perhaps it is not true."

"Yes, is it true, just you wait, she has been seen out for dinner several times with him so watch this space," said Freddie smiling.

She told Gemma and Freddie about her lunch and that it looked like they would get the tour.

"Gemma if it comes off and you haven't any other work booked that you have to personally oversee perhaps you would like to be tour manager; it would mean you staying at each location for four days a week for the whole of the tour, what do you think?"

"Mum, I would love it, so fingers crossed that it comes off. As soon as you hear confirmation let me help you with the arrangements, I can do the recce in the shopping centres which would save you from all that travelling and if I am to be the tour manager it will give me the opportunity of meeting everyone involved before the show visits."

A week later they had confirmation from Ford about the tour that it would go ahead, but Carl said that they would have to have another meeting before the dealership events could be signed off.

Gemma and Annabel started to work on the logistics of the tour which turned out to be rather complicated but working together did help. Gemma made appointments to visit those centres that had the highest footfall with a good spread across the country so that they covered as much as possible. She had also contacted a logistics company who she had heard was very good to speak about the set and lighting that needed to be erected and the placement of the cars in the designated space.

They now had in the office a very comprehensive file on shopping centres with all the data that a client would need, so Annabel decided that she would approach some more companies to see if they would be interested in roadshows, but first she had to get this show 'on the road.'

Gemma reported back after her visit that she wanted to use the logistics company and that they would prepare for them detailed drawings of the promotional area to show the management of each centre.

Freddie got to work on booking promotional staff for each venue and a hotel for Gemma in each city, so it looked like all the loose ends were being tied up.

Annabel had worked in London nonstop now for the whole week and felt like a break but decided before she went home, she would call Shawn to thank him for the beautiful flowers. She went into her office to make the call as speaking to a man in front of Gemma was not a good idea. She rang the mobile number that she had been given but it went straight to voice mail, so she just left a message saying thank you for the flowers. Within five minutes her phone rang.

"Hello, Annie's Agency."

"Hello Annabel, this is Shawn Rogers, sorry I was not

available to take your call before."

"No problem, I just wanted to say thank you for the beautiful flowers and apologise for not calling before, but things have been really busy."

There was a pause before Shawn spoke again as if he was unsure of what to say next.

"I am just leaving for the day and wondered if you have the time, that you might like to join me for a drink."

"That sounds lovely, a drink is just what I need after the day I have had. Where would you like to meet?"

They arranged to meet in the bar at the Ritz Hotel in half an hour so Annabel tided up her desk and said that she was going back to Portsmouth, she caught a taxi outside her office and arrived just at the same time as Shawn.

"Good timing," he said as he took her arm as they entered the hotel.

After they had found seats and ordered the drinks Annabel looked at this man she had agreed to meet, he really was most attractive perhaps a little too old for her but very charming and had perfect manners.

"Well Annabel, tell me about yourself, I know about the work you are involved in but nothing about you."

Annabel told him how she had started the agency and about the first contract that she had lost to a competitor and how angry she was which had prompted her to open her own office.

"Carrying anger around with you is not good, you should think about the opportunity that she gave you; you might still be sharing an office with her now but for the loss of that show. Do you know what she is doing now? Is she still in the business?"

"I had heard that she does very little work here in this country, but some shows in Europe, so it does not sound like her business is going well."

"Just think Annabel your revenge was to go on to become successful, in a way thanks to her. I firmly believe that what you do comes back, good or bad. Forget about that woman and move on."

Shawn told her that he had been brought up in Ireland and moved over to England when he was just 10 years old. His father was a doctor which had prompted him to go into medicine and then specialise. He owned a home outside Dublin and visited it for family holidays.

They talked about their families and the two children he had of which he was very proud; his daughter was also in medicine and was a surgeon at the Middlesex Hospital specialising in paediatrics and his son was a barrister. He said that his wife spent much of her time in Ireland as she was an author and liked the peace that she found there.

It was so nice thought Annabel to find someone who is interested in hearing about other people and not just wanting to talk about themselves. She wanted to know more about this man and to spend time with him.

When they were ready to leave Shawn asked her if she would like to meet for lunch the following week as there was a new restaurant that he wanted to try, and he thought that she might enjoy it.

"I would very much like to meet with you again, thank you for asking me."

On the train back home, she thought about the pleasant hour she had spent with Shawn. Looking out the window as the train sped to Portsmouth her thoughts went to Oliver and the last time she had seen him, when he was standing on the station platform. She still missed him so much and hoped that he was well and happy. He had been such a special person in her life and in leaving he had left such a big hole both in her life and in her heart.

Chapter Thirty-Four
On the Road

The roadshows had started the tour, and Gemma reported back weekly with the data that they had captured for Ford and also which promotional girls she thought that they should use again, and which ones were lazy and should be taken off the books. She said that the logistics company they were using was really good and it sounded like Gemma had started dating the owner and was enjoying her time with him. They were both free and single so why not?

The Daily Mail had by this time taken over the ownership of the Ski Shows and wanted the agency to pitch for the 'Fantasia' part of the show. She was very excited about this and had prepared an exciting proposal which she had to give to the board at their head office the following week, but now she was getting ready to meet Shawn for lunch.

The restaurant that Shawn had chosen was in Knightsbridge and looked very elegant. She gave the name of who she was meeting and was shown to a table overlooking the pretty gardens. Shawn stood as she approached the table.

"How nice to see you again and thank you for meeting me."

"It's my pleasure, this beats eating a sandwich at my desk any day."

They studied the menu and gave their choices to the waiter

and then they both started to speak at once which broke the ice and they started laughing.

"Tell me Annabel, what is it you like to do when you are not working."

"Well, I seem to be spending much of my time checking on my children who all have different needs, but when I have free time, I love listening to music. In fact, when we have finished lunch, I am going to buy a new sound system for my apartment as the one I have is broken. I also enjoy horse riding but unfortunately, I have not had much time lately to go out on a ride but I have promised myself that I am going to call the local stables this weekend to book a morning out. So, if you see me next week, I probably will not be able to walk as it has been such a long time since I have been on a horse, I will be hurting in places I didn't know I had."

"I also enjoy riding, are you ever in town on the weekend, if so, I would like to take you to the country there are beautiful rides there and the local stables I use have some fine horses."

"Well not this weekend, as I already have plans I cannot change but the following weekend would be perfect."

Shawn had to take a telephone call during the meal and when he had finished talking asked if she would excuse him for a moment as he had to make a call but said he would only be a moment.

The meal was superb as was Shawn's company, as they got up to leave, he asked if she was in a hurry as he wanted to collect something from Harrods. She said that she was not in a rush so would come with him as she loved the store and just liked to look around even if she didn't buy anything.

They walked to Harrods which was only a short distance from the restaurant and Shawn led her to a lift as he what needed was on the second floor. When Shawn walked over to the desk, she thought that she would walk around to see if she could find a small sound system that she needed to buy.

In a short while Shawn came over to where Annabel was standing carrying a box in one of the famous Harrods green carrier bags.

"Come on I have taken enough of your time, let me find you a taxi so you can be on your way."

They left the store and Shawn hailed her a taxi and opened the door so she could climb in and then put the box he was carrying on the floor by her feet.

"Just something for you to use, I will call you next week to arrange our day in the country," and with that he closed the door.

Annabel opened the bag and saw that the box contained a top of the range sound system, she was flabbergasted with the extraordinary generous gift and now was embarrassed. How could she except this? She quickly made a call to his mobile.

"I hope you like what I have chosen for you," said Shawn as he answered

"Shawn, I did not mention that I wanted a sound system so you could buy me one."

"No Annabel, I know you didn't, it is just nice to think that you will be able to continue to enjoy your music and to thank you for joining me today."

Annabel asked the taxi to stop first at the apartment so that she could leave the box before continuing to Waterloo station.

What a lovely and generous man thought Annabel, and she was looking forward to seeing him again next week.

....

She arrived at the head office of the Mail and was shown straight into the boardroom. There were about eight people sitting round the table, David the Editor got up to welcome her and to introduce her to the rest of the board, some of them she had already met and she said hello before sitting down to present her proposal.

"I have broken the show down into five different scenes each with a different theme and will highlight each one with either a group skiing or aerialists, the Swiss couple that I know you have contracted will perform a scene from *Phantom of the Opera* with if possible an organ coming up from beneath the slope, but the finale will be the highlight with all the performers taking part and I would love to have some of my dancers on a trapeze if these can be rigged either side of the slope so we will have a circus theme with some of the skiers dressed as clowns.

"All the music will have performing rights applied for, but we will need a budget for the special outfits to be made such as the cloak for the Phantom scene and clowns and trapeze artists for the finale. The cost of the stage effects has still to be finalised, but I can let you have them shortly."

When she had finished speaking, she got up from her chair to hand round a bound book to each person with both the proposal and the cost. As she sat down again, she said with a smile.

"My case rests."

There was silence for a few moments until a round of applause was made.

She felt confident that she had made a good impression and hopefully she would be considered to produce the

'Fantasia.' She would just have to wait until she heard back from them.

Later that afternoon she received a call from the organiser of the ski show, she hoped that it wasn't bad news.

"Annabel thank you for coming in today. You presented your proposal really well and everyone has agreed that they would like you to be awarded the contract, so well done."

What fantastic news, that would mean that at the next Ski Exhibition she would produce both the Fashion Show as well as the Ski Fantasia and she had also just heard that the agency had been awarded the contract for the fashion show at the Caravan and Camping exhibition which was being held on the ground floor of the Exhibition halls at the same time, so her work would really be cut out for her during that time.

She went out to buy some Champagne and lots of goodies to eat so that Freddie and anyone that came in that afternoon could help celebrate with them.

It was such a noisy happy time with models coming in all afternoon, she had telephoned Alan the choreographer to tell him to come in as well as Lottie from upstairs. Models who had heard on the grapevine and wanted to be part of the agency's success popped in for a glass of Champagne and she soon had to send out for more supplies, it was a myth to say that models didn't drink or eat much.

She telephoned Gemma who was still away on tour and sent a message through to David, Barry, Poppy and Simon who were also delighted for her. In fact, everyone she knew had a call from her.

She found a quiet moment to call through to Shawn who she hoped was not busy with a patient, but he answered immediately.

"Annabel that is such good news, I am so happy for you. Now we really have something to celebrate so I think after our ride we will go to the Le Manoir Aux Quart Saisons restaurant. What do you think?"

"I think that that would be perfect and as I am staying in town over that weekend there is no reasons to rush, so thank you."

A reason to be happy thought Annabel as she put down the phone.

Chapter Thirty-Five
Shawn

Annabel had been collected from her apartment in Baker Street by Shawn early on Saturday morning and she had managed to find her jodhpurs and hat and was wearing a thick sweater over her shirt but had brought a change of clothes for when they went out later for dinner.

Shawn was driving a sports car, so she put her bag in the boot as it was only a two-seater and settled down for the drive to the Cotswolds where the stables that Shawn used were located. The drive was lovely as he did not use the motorway but passed through some picturesque villages, as the ride was not booked till midday, they even had time to stop on the way for a coffee.

Apart from the last weekend Annabel had not been out on a horse for quite some time so it was quite a thrill to arrive at the very well-maintained stables and have an opportunity to look around. She had some mints in her pocket so she could make friends with her horse. She had told Shawn that she was really only a novice as she had been riding for two years and did not like to take any jumps, but a gallop would be fine.

"Don't worry I will look after you and make sure that you don't come to any harm, and the horse I have chosen for you, is very good-tempered."

The horses that they were using were brought out for them

already tacked up so after Annabel had mounted, she adjusted the stirrups and tightened the girth, and then proceeded to walk round the yard to get a feel for her horse. When they were ready Shawn led the way out of the yard and as they were taking the horses out on their own, she followed behind.

The first part of the ride was just walking and a gentle canter when they could, when Shawn saw that Annabel seemed comfortable, he asked her if she felt ready for a gallop. "Go for it."

They took off along a path which went through a large wood and Shawn had obviously listened to her about jumps as they did not come up against any gates. it was invigorating with the wind blowing against her face and only the sounds of the horses' hooves to disturb the silence, it was the best feeling in the world, no one speaking to her, no phones ringing and no complaints from models. They rode like this for a while until they came to a stream when Shawn slowed down to a walk

"Let us dismount and let our friends have a little drink."

It was cool in the woods and she shivered as the wind had a chill to it.

"Annabel take my sweater; I don't want you to get cold."

Shawn took off his sweater and put it round her while putting his arms around her body. They were standing so close and as he looked at Annabel he bent down and gently kissed her lips.

Annabel looked at his face when he had pulled back and put her own arms round his neck so that she could pull him nearer to her and kiss him some more.

They stood like this for a while just enjoying the closeness of each other and kissing without any hurry, they heard the horses neighing as if they wanted some more fun so reluctantly, they pulled apart and mounted again to resume their ride but this time just walking side by side so that they could talk.

After several hours having had a good gallop back through the woods, they arrived at the stables. It had been a perfect afternoon, and now they were on their way to the restaurant, but a feeling of closeness enveloped them both as they held hands on the drive.

The hotel and restaurant were tucked away in the picturesque countryside and had two Michelin stars awarded to it and as Annabel had never eaten there she was looking forward to the evening.

"Shawn I will need a little time to wash and change when we get to the hotel as I want to look good for you and at the moment, I feel like a mess."

"You would never look a mess to me, but don't worry I will book a room for you to change and will wait for you downstairs."

This man was so lovely thought Annabel as she had a quick shower, redid her makeup brushed her hair and changed into the clothes that she had brought with her, and when she was ready joined Shawn in the bar.

"I left my bag with reception so don't let me forget it when we leave and thank you for organising a room for me."

"Anything that makes you happy," said Shawn as he took her hand and twined his fingers with hers.

They were shown into the main restaurant and seated at a table with garden views, the selection on the menu was enticing and Annabel realised that after the ride she was really hungry.

"Shawn, there is so much to choose from, why don't you

make the selection for me?" He studied the menu for a while and then gave the order to the waiter. The meal was exceptional, and they spent a relaxing evening together. It was an opportunity to find out more about this interesting man that she was so lucky to have met.

"You talk very little about your family, your children and your wife, I don't want to pry but I am interested in you, in your life. I know that you are a very successful specialist but I know so little about you, where you live what your interests are?"

Shawn sat back and waited a moment before he began to speak.

"Well, Annabel, my life is quite ordinary, like most people my age I am married with a family. I have been married for nearly 30 years, my wife and I met when we were both working for the NHS, she was working with the paediatric team as a nurse but gave it up when we married to look after our family. She unfortunately has suffered with bad health and was advised to take things at a much slower pace, so she took up writing and spends much of her time at our home in Ireland. I try and get out there as much as possible as it is a beautiful country and it restores the soul just being there.

"I have told you that I have two children who I am very proud they both live in London, my son is married and has a child while my daughter is single, she tells me that the perfect man has not come along yet.

"We live in Bath and have a lovely Georgian house there and if my wife is in England I always travel back, at other times I stay at my club in Knightsbridge, she is coming back in the morning so that is why I cannot be too late as I have a long drive ahead of me tonight."

"Shawn you should have said we could have left much earlier."

"I didn't want to spoil this lovely day we have spent together, but if you have finished perhaps, we should be on our way."

Shawn paid the bill and they collected Annabel's bag from reception before heading off to the motorway for the drive back to London.

Annabel told him about her own family and the home she had in Portsmouth and how she had started her agency many years ago. The time seemed to fly by as they talked but arriving back in Baker Street Shawn parked his car and turned off the ignition.

"We seem to have so much to tell each other and so little time to do it we will have to arrange to meet soon."

He leaned forward to take Annabel in his arms and his kisses were hard against her mouth as if he could not get enough. They sat like that for many minutes.

"My sweet Annabel, I must go and if I don't leave now, I might find I cannot leave at all. I want to feel you, all of you, to spend time exploring your body but the first time we are together must not be here in a car like teenagers but to have the time to make it special for both of us."

They leaned forward to kiss a final time and after Annabel had collected her bag, she stood on the pavement watching as Shawn drove away.

Chapter Thirty-Six
Newspaper Launch

Gemma and Annabel were sitting at a meeting with a PR company who had been asked to organise the launch of a new daily free newspaper called *The Mezzo* and had asked the agency if they could provide the staff.

"The launch will start here in London where we can evaluate the success and iron out any glitches and then it will be rolled out across the country; Birmingham, Manchester Newcastle, Glasgow and Edinburgh.

"We need at least 150 staff a day five days a week in each location to hand out the paper at major stations, perhaps more in London as we must cover the tube stations as well. When permission is given for the paper to be put into bins to be collected by commuters, we will then not need so many staff, but this could take many months.

"We know this is not your usual type of work, but you come highly recommended as you have a reputation of being reliable and hardworking. What we need to know is if you are interested in being part of this promotion as it is very large scale, and most importantly if you can handle these very large numbers."

"I can assure you that I would not take on any work if I felt unsure about any aspect of it. I need to know that you will be able to let me have all the details with as much notice as you are able to give us."

Annabel loved a challenge but needed a few days to discuss how they would handle the promotion before coming back with a detailed proposal, so it was arranged to meet again early next week when she had had a chance to play with the numbers.

Gemma and Annabel went straight back to the office to discuss how this could be worked without impinging on their main business.

"We need to set up a complete new division to handle this and I think I will organise this from Portsmouth, I can use the barn at home as an office as Barry has now moved into a flat with his girlfriend so it is empty. We will need an administrator based in the office and a technical manager to oversee the delivery of the papers each day and to run a programme so all the data can be stored.

"Gemma I can organise the administration of the promotion but you will need to find the staff and managers in each city, if you think you can handle that side I am sure we can confirm that we can deliver."

"Mum, we can get students who are always looking to find work so that will not be a problem and if we can pay them at the end of each week word will soon go out that we are looking for staff — say yes."

This was a big contract and needed some time to organise all the various aspects but with a good team behind them they could provide the staff and deliver the promotion.

The following few days were hectic as Annabel needed to make sure her costings included everything that they could possibly need, so she spent much time going over the figures while Gemma made calls to universities, student unions and various clubs to ask if they would put up posters advertising that staff were needed, she also visited some local schools where they had a sixth form.

By the time of the next meeting Annabel felt that she had a good handle on the administration side but before they could start booking both the staff and the managers she needed written confirmation that the agency had the contract and that the fee she needed was agreeable, she also needed to have funds in the bank in advance at the start of each week.

Everyone was happy when the meeting came to a close and the PR company assured Annabel that as soon as the newspaper confirmed the start date, she would have everything she needed from them. A full back-up from them would be available.

Gemma had started to make calls for staff and had sent through posters advertising that staff were wanted daily and so far she had had an excellent response back and it looked like they were able certainly in London to fill the numbers of staff needed, which was 850 staff a day at all tube and mainline stations. For the moment she was just concentrating on the London area as that was the crucial part of the roll out. She also spent each evening visiting pubs and clubs to spread the word and had appointed some team leaders who were taking the calls and listing names and numbers and a daily meeting was held back at the office to collate all the information

Poor Freddie was besieged by strange people calling in while still managing to run the model and dancers' side of the business. He seemed to thrive on this crazy time and had given Gemma some names of gay clubs to contact as he said that were many young men out of work at this time and he was sure that they would be able to help. They spent long hours at the office and Freddie, bless him, stayed late as well to lend a hand.

....

The first day at Waterloo Station arrived and the system they had put in place seemed to be working well, as since 5am when the papers had been dropped there was a hive of activity at each tube and mainline station. Gemma and her team leaders were going between stations to check on staff and the number of copies of the paper they were able to hand out and to request more if needed or transfer the staff to other stations where they were needed more.

There were a few 'no shows' at some stations and the team quickly deployed staff from other venues to cover while making calls to have extra staff available to work.

Gemma had found at one tube station that the papers had been dumped instead of being given out, and the staff had gone home, how did those people think that they were being paid for not doing any work. She called through to the Portsmouth office and told Lesley the new administrator to not pay them and to take them off the list for any future work. She also told Lesley that she had taken a photo of the papers in a bin in case they disputed not receiving any wages, and if they turned up tomorrow morning to send them home.

By the second day many more staff had contacted the team leaders saying that they were available for work and a comprehensive list was drawn up to use. London was certainly a winner. Everyone who had been handed a paper were happy to receive it with only very few declining to take a free copy.

At the end of the week Annabel and Gemma took all the

team leaders out for a drink and a meal to thank them for all their hard work and to find out which ones might be willing to relocate to Manchester as they now had the confirmation that the city was next on the list. All expenses were being paid and there was a bonus if each person was able to recruit staff and deliver the numbers of the newspaper that would be delivered.

Annabel was confident that the team that they had put in place were working well and with Gemma setting up in each city and then making spot visits she could now concentrate on the forthcoming shows at the exhibitions.

There was much to organise as she had three shows going on at one venue which would be hard going, and she needed a clear head to concentrate on these.

She had spoken to Shawn a few times but they had been unable to meet up as he was travelling back to Bath most nights and with the newspaper launch she did not have time during the day, but they had arranged a date when they were both free and Annabel had said that instead of going out she would cook a meal for them both and promised that her cooking was good enough to pass even his exacting standards.

"Please don't go to too much trouble, I am happy with whatever you serve me, and we could always order in."

"No way, it will be my pleasure to invite you over and cook for you. Just turn up hungry." After she had finished the call she was smiling. It would be so nice to see him again and he would be the visitor she had in her apartment.

Chapter Thirty-Seven
A Night to Remember

After Annabel had finished work for the day, she went out to shop for the meal she was going to make for Shawn. It was fun organising a dinner menu as she had not entertained any of her friends for such a long time and when the children were home, they liked very basic food so her culinary skills were not put too much use.

She had decided to make a delicious turkey roasted in lemon, orange, and tangerine juice, and stuffed with meat, roasted chestnuts and pine nuts and served with oven-roasted vegetables. She had prepared an avocado, tomato and mozzarella cheese starter and just a fresh fruit salad to finish.

She tidied up the apartment and set the table in the kitchen with her best wine, water glasses and cutlery and arranged a pretty arrangement of flowers in the centre. She put all the table lamps on low and closed the curtains, music was playing softly on her new sound system that Shawn had given her and now that the main course was in the oven cooking and the starter in the fridge ready to be served all was ready and now it was time to make herself beautiful for Shawn.

She had chosen a new silk dress that she had bought from her designer friend and teamed it with stockings and high heels, a quick spray of her favourite perfume Joy and she was ready just as the front doorbell rang. She pushed the entry bell as she answered, "please come in, I am on the top floor."

She went to open the door and saw just the top of Shawn's head as he was carrying an enormous bunch of flowers in one hand and a carrier bag in the other. As he reached the top of the stairs, he handed Annabel the flowers which she saw were at least two dozen of the most beautiful red roses.

"I thought that I would provide the wine," he said as he closed the door behind him and took off his coat and placed a kiss on her face.

"Come in, let me put these flowers in water and then I can show you around."

Shawn loved the apartment and complemented Annabel on her flair with the decorations and furniture.

"This is just lovely, if I were to have an apartment in town, I would like it to be exactly like this," he said.

Annabel took one of the bottles that Shawn had brought and laid two glasses and an opener on the coffee table in the lounge. When they were seated, he opened the wine and poured them each a glass.

They were sitting very close together on the couch, his arm was round her shoulders and his fingers were playing with her neck which was sending little bolts of electricity through her.

Annabel put her glass on the coffee table and put both her arms round his neck and slowly kissed him; his eyes, his head, his nose and then his beautiful lips She could taste the wine and it tasted so sweet on his mouth. His tongue went inside her mouth moving it slowly round and then he put his tongue inside her ears and gently traced her ear lopes and moved his mouth so he could give them small bites.

Their passionate, deep, amorous kisses were igniting

feelings in each other by touching their tongues to each other's lips and inside their mouths they could feel the heat raising through their bodies, his hands on her body touching her was making it hard to pull away, but she wanted take things a little slower, she did not want to rush this special moment the first time that they could be together.

She pulled away still holding on to him and looking into his eyes and could see that Shawn felt the same. Why rush when they had all night to explore each other, to find out what pleasured them to make love not to just have sex?

"Do you like my music?" asked Annabel as she caressed his face and the dulcet tones of Leonard Cohen could be heard.

"I like everything about you, what you do, what you say is all that I could want in a woman, and you are very special."

"Come Shawn let me feed you first and then you can tell me what you really like."

They went into the kitchen and Shawn sat at the table while Annabel served up the meal, they tried to take a leisurely pace and eat slowly and savour the wine, but it was hard as both of them wanted to touch each other and feel close and when eating just didn't feel important anymore. Shawn took Annabel's hand and led her into the bedroom where he began to undress her slowly.

Taking of her dress until she was only in her underwear, he stood back to admire her, and then undid her bra and took off her pants until she only had on stockings and her high heel shoes. she stood very still while his hands touched her body as if he had to remember every part of her and commit it to memory.

When she could stand it no longer, she reached forwards to undress him, throwing his clothes onto the floor. They stood like this for a few moments until with a sigh that seemed to come from somewhere deep inside him, he picked Annabel up and gently laid her on the bed moving his body above hers and slowly put his penis against her, moving forwards until the tip was just touching that special part of her. She was wet with just the thought of him, she wanted to feel every part of his manhood so that he could fill her up with his juices and they could become one.

"Now please Shawn, I want you inside of me, all of you."

He moved very slowly until she could feel him filling up that space with his body. His movements became more hurried as he pushed harder and with every thrust Annabel could feel herself reacting as a warm feeling enveloped her body and her skin became sensitive to his touch, her heart was racing and then the release as they reached that joyous time and came together in a magical moment. Annabel had never felt such happiness as she did at that moment as if all the stars in the sky had exploded in her and her soul, mind and body were one with him.

They lay together on the bed breathing slowly until her heart had slowed down and she could see that Shawn was looking at her and smiling.

They did not need any words to express how they felt, they had waited a long time for this and wanted to relish every moment.

Annabel traced her fingers across his chest and down his belly until she could feel his cock wet with her juices, she played with him until she could feel him move beneath her hand and his cock start to harden. She moved her lips above him and took him in her mouth moving her tongue round him and with her hand she took his balls and gently stroked them.

She could feel his whole body stiffen beneath her as he pushed her onto her back and started to kiss her.

He kissed her face and then moved down to her breasts and sucked on her nipples while his fingers played inside her vagina making her feel that she was ready again to take him inside her.

They played like this with each other until he pushed inside her with great hard thrusts, and they came to climax which seemed to be even better than before.

Time seemed to stand still as they rested on the bed, hands clasped and her head in his arms enjoying this moment of peace.

The dawn was rising through the windows of the bedroom when they stirred and as Annabel opened her eyes, she could see that Shawn was awake.

"Would you like me to run you a bath, or perhaps you might prefer a shower?"

"Anything as long as you take it with me."

Annabel filled the bath with her most expensive foam she could find in her cupboard and they both climbed into the bath, Shawn laid back against the end of the bath while Annabel soaped his body with a sponge and when they were finished, they wrapped each other in warm towels and went through to the lounge.

She made them both a coffee and sat in each other's arms, not speaking just enjoying being together.

"Annabel I must go as I need to change my clothes at my club as I do not think arriving at my consulting rooms like this would go down very well with my patients, and my nurse would not be very impressed."

Annabel quickly tidied the room while Shawn got

dressed.

"When will I see you again?" asked Shawn as he stood ready to leave.

"Call me later and we can arrange something. I am staying here in London for the next few days as I have three shows to organise so even if you only have time for a quick coffee that would be good."

Shawn kissed her on her lips as he opened the door and with a last look went downstairs.

Annabel looked round the kitchen which looked like a disaster area with the remains of their half-eaten meal still on the table. She put everything she could salvage in the fridge and threw the rest away. She arranged her roses into two vases in the lounge which looked beautiful and was a reminder of the lovely night they had spent.

She dressed quickly and after collecting her briefcase made her way to the office.

Chapter Thirty-Eight
The 'Fantasia'

The fashion show at the Ski Show was in rehearsals and the stage set that was being built at the bottom of the slope looked amazing. Alan the choreographer had also organised the rehearsals for the Caravan and Camping Show that would open just a few days later.

Annabel's main focus was the Ski Fantasia and she had called together all the skiers and aerialists to discuss the format of the show and play the music that they would be using so that they had a good feel for it. The actual jumps that were to be made had to be on split second timing as there was much going on, on the slope and organising the various activities both on the slope and the ramp needed to be rehearsed so that all the cast knew their cues.

"As you know we are using the music from the West End show *Phantom of the Opera* for one of the scenes which the owners of the exhibition want us to include, so skiers must be aware of the organ that will rise up from under the slope, and the finale will have skiers, aerialists, dancers and trapeze artists all on at the same time so be careful that you take your marks and that you perform exactly where you have been told and not move off into another area.

"We have arranged all the costumes for fittings in a room behind the organiser's office so can you please make your way over there now and any costumes that need to be altered can be done."

Annabel went over to the sound engineers' box to check that he was OK and that the paperwork for the performing rights licence that they needed to play the music had been taken out.

After all her checks had been done, she made her way over to where the fittings were being held and she could hear much noise as she opened the door.

One of the aerialists was standing in the middle of the room wearing his finale costume but when she looked, she saw that as he was a rather big boy and his jock strap was much too small. The whole room was collapsed in laughter as he paraded up and down showing off. When she stopped laughing herself and could speak, she asked if he wanted a new costume made or did, he feel he would make more of an impact if he just wore it as it was!

The cast were a great bunch; champions from all over the world in their various fields and she was looking forward to working with them. She was very excited about the spectacular as it was the first of its kind; a West End show performed on a ski slope.

She had spoken to Shawn and asked if he would like tickets for the Ski Exhibition as she had been told she could invite guests into the VIP lounge which overlooked the slope.

"Annabel I would love to see what you do so why don't I come over tomorrow evening after the opening and perhaps we can go for a drink after you have finished?"

The first day was pandemonium with exhibitors frantically trying to finish their stands for when the doors opened to the public. The press had already been in to take photos of the main stars of the show and both the models and dancers were in the dressing room getting ready for the show.

At last a bell sounded which was the signal for the doors to be opened and the exhibition to start. First on the stage was the fashion show, the lights dimmed and the music started and an explosion of smoke covered the stage and suddenly the public could see the dancers come out from what looked like openings in a rock face covered in snow, they were all wearing the latest ski fashions and dancing to songs from, Michael Jackson, Take That, The Beatles and M People. The whole hall vibrated with the sound and the atmosphere was electric.

Thunderous applause greeted each scene and when the show was finished, the head of marketing from the company whose clothes they were showing, came over to Annabel to congratulate her and the team for a fabulous show.

Now it was time for the Fantasia. Annabel had gone backstage to speak to all the cast and said that she would be out front and rooting for them. The two dancers who were going to perform on the trapeze were already in place above the slope. She was pleased that it wasn't her that had to climb up as she remembered that last time she had tried and what a disaster it had been.

An announcement came over the tannoy system to ask the public to please make their way to the slope as the Fantasia was about to begin.

The Fantasia was all that Annabel had hoped it would be; exciting, thrilling and spectacular. The organ rose from the slope without any mishap, the cast performed wonderfully, and the circus finale was fantastic. The whole of the board of the Mail were there and were delighted with the show.

Annabel spent the rest of the day making sure that

everyone was OK and that they had enough to eat and drink between performances. She was now waiting for Shawn to arrive. She had told him about the work the agency did, but this would be the first time he had seen anything.

She was waiting in the VIP lounge when Shawn was shown up.

"My God what a crowd. How do you manage to stay sane with all this going on each day?"

"It's all part of the industry I work in, so I am used to it now," said Annabel smiling. She wanted to give him a hug but thought that as so many people were around that it was not a good idea. Instead she offered him a drink from the bar and just touched his fingers lightly as she handed the glass to him.

"Come, the show is about to begin, and it is the reason you came this evening so stand here by me so you can have a good view."

"It's not the only reason I came over, but while I am here, I would like to see what you do."

Shawn loved the show and clapped hard when it had finished and told her how much he had enjoyed the spectacular and how impressed he was with what she had produced.

"Do you want to look round the exhibition before we leave? Or would you like to go now?"

"Let's leave, as it is very hard to be close but not touch you."

Annabel led Shawn down to the basement where her car was parked as he had come over by taxi from Harley Street. As they got in the car they kissed and ran their hands over each other as there was not a lot of room to do much else. She drove out of the car park and headed for a small bar she knew not far away.

He was smiling at her as they sat nursing their drinks.

"What's the matter? Have I got dirt on my face?"

"No, I can see some writing on your forehead. Do you want to know what it says?"

Annabel looked surprised, what was he talking about

"It says, 'Fuck me,' but only I can read it."

Annabel laughed, that was just what she wanted to do but she was so tired she could just about keep her eyes open.

"Shawn do you think that if I promise not to wash my face and keep the message there until tomorrow for you, we can do it then?"

"Yes, my darling girl, I can see how wiped out you are but before you go, I have a small gift for you."

He handed over a small box which was tied up with a red ribbon and had the name Cartier on it. She undid the ribbon and opened the box to see a beautiful Cartier watch inside.

"This is just to remind you never to be late to meet me."

"Oh, Shawn you spoil me. I don't deserve someone like you but thank you darling it is a wonderful present and I am going to wear it immediately."

She took off her own and put the watch on her wrist and kept looking at this marvellous gift.

"Thank you, thank you and I am sorry about cutting short this evening but I have to be up really early tomorrow as the Caravan and Camping exhibition opens and I need all my wits about me with three shows to organise."

They said goodbye outside the bar and Shawn hailed a taxi to take him back to his club while Annabel headed off to Baker Street for a bath and bed.

The Caravan Show opened without incident and both the shows at the ski exhibition were running smoothly when she was called into a meeting in the organiser's office. Not really knowing what to expect she wasn't unduly concerned until she entered the office to see both David the editor and the show organiser looking very irritated and angry.

"Sit down Annabel, I have just heard from the Really Useful Company who own *The Phantom of the Opera* and they have threatened to close us down unless we pay them a very large amount of money to continue to use that scene in our show."

"I am sorry David, but we have the performing rights licence which gives us the right to use the music, I don't understand what the problem is."

"The problem is that we did not obtain the artistic rights."

Annabel did not understand what was being said as she had never heard about 'artistic rights' having to be obtained.

"If we had worn the Phantom's mask on the other side of his face, we would have been OK but because it was an exact copy, they want to sue. The newspaper has agreed to pay which means that the balance of your fee is not going to be paid to you."

There wasn't anything that Annabel could say, she could not fight the newspaper or the company who owned the rights she just had to accept that she would be blamed and not be paid the full amount that had been agreed. She felt that she was being made a scapegoat for an issue that was not her fault, but it sounded like the newspaper wanted to save face by having someone take the blame. She had never been in a situation like this before. It felt like a scene from a bad movie

As she got up to leave, David opened the door for her, and said quietly, "I am sorry Annabel it has been taken out of my hands, but I promise that I will have to make sure that somehow we make it up to you."

Annabel felt sick but there was nothing to do but accept the decision. She was fortunate that with three shows running she had enough money to pay everyone it would just mean that her profit would be less and would have to careful on what she spent over the next few months.

She didn't want to stay around but had to see everyone before she left. She needed a few days away from the exhibition so decided to go home for the weekend to catch her breath and get some rest.

She wanted someone to talk to, but she didn't want to bother Shawn with this as she knew he was operating that day and David was away and wouldn't understand. He didn't seem to take much interest in her or her work at the moment. They seemed to have drifted apart even more over the last few months and was something they needed to talk about when he was home next on leave.

She was cross and upset and felt like crying but that was the joy of running your own business; the ups and downs were all part of the package and she had to shoulder on and keep smiling.

Chapter Thirty-Nine
Trouble

Annabel received a call from the Manchester team at Mezzo as they all sounded stressed out. She thought that she needed to visit which was why she was sitting on a train early in the evening heading up to the city.

Jeffery who oversaw the promotion had made his base at the hotel and was causing havoc. He was insisting on changing the way the promotion was run. He stayed in his room he had set up as his headquarters without visiting the depots or staff. What he was requesting was imposable to organise at such short notice.

When Annabel entered his room all she could see was chaos; half-eaten sandwiches, cups with cold coffee and papers scattered everywhere. There were several other people in the room either taking notes or typing on laptops and mobile phones seemed to be ringing constantly.

Jeffery was pacing up and down the room shouting at the top of his voice

"I am in charge! You will do what I say, or you will be sacked immediately. I will not have this nonsense from anybody," with that he finished the call and threw his phone down. When he saw Annabel standing in the doorway he snapped, "what do you want? Go away. I'm busy."

"Jeffery, I am Annabel from the agency who is handling

the promotion and I am here to see what I can do to help as you seem to be concerned about the way we are working."

"Too bloody right I am concerned. I don't like your manager or the staff you are providing, and I want you to find new people immediately. This promotion has to run the way I want, and if I say jump, you jump, do you understand?" he shouted prodding his finger into Annabel's shoulder so he could make his point better.

Annabel could see that she would not have any success in trying to talk to this man who seemed to be out of control. Making a call back to the head office of the PR company this late in the day was out of the question, so she said that she would visit the depot and talk to the manager and perhaps they could meet early the next morning to talk through exactly what he wanted to change.

"I want you to be here at 5 a.m. and if I have the time, we will have a meeting. In the meantime, I will send you my instructions either by email or text whenever I need to, which you have to respond to immediately. Do you understand?" He then turned away to take another call.

What a horrible man thought Annabel, how on earth had he been put in charge to run things when he had no idea of what was needed or how things worked?

She went up to the room the team leaders were using and found several of the team sleeping either on the bed or floor; wherever there was space. Gemma had told her that morale was low because of Jeffery and she had arranged for some of the team to have a massage to relax them. The only problem was that they had fallen asleep on the massage table and were reluctant to wake up, so the therapists had left them there to sleep.

"I am going out to visit the depot now so you rest here, and I will meet with Jeffery in the morning to try and try and talk some sense into him."

Just at that moment her mobile rang with a message and when she looked, she saw it was from Jeffery, the message was written in large capital letters.

'SACK ALL THE STAFF. I WANT NEW PEOPLE WORKING IN THE MORNING.'

Well, that was not going to happen, thought Annabel, as since he won't leave his room, he would not really know who was working, and how was she supposed to find another 150 staff to work within four hours? She didn't know. She had total faith in the manager and knew the crew who were working were good kids; turning up on time and working hard to hand out the paper.

At the depot she found that all was running well but the head office of the paper had requested 50 more staff to work that night and for the rest of that week as they had a special promotion on. She sent the team leaders to the hotel kitchens and student bars to see if they could recruit more staff at that late hour and promised a £10 cash bonus to anyone who came back with the extra people, even if she could not use them that night there would be work for them in the coming days

At 5 a.m. she presented herself to Jeffery and she saw that in the time she had been away his temper had not cooled. He still looked incandescent with rage.

"What exactly would you like us to do Jeffery so that we can organise the promotion that fits in with your brief?"

"Well, I want the managers to report to me as soon as they have finished their shift for the day and fill out reports so I can see what they have been doing. And if I am not happy, they

216

will have to stay here until I am satisfied, do you understand?"

"Jeffery what you are asking is not going to be possible as when they have finished they need to check the papers that are left and call the newspaper to give them the numbers, then check with all the staff that have worked that they have handed in their dockets to make sure that all numbers are correct and then call our office in Portsmouth to log those people in as having worked. Next, they have to make calls for the following day for the people we need; all that while trying to get home, eat and sleep before they start again.

"I don't care about them sleeping. They can sleep when they have finished working for me or they will not be working at all, and I don't like your manager as he has an attitude and told me he only answers to you."

"Jeffery, he hasn't met with you and so the only person he knows and has to repot to is me. But I suggest you accompany me tomorrow morning so you can see how we are working and then you can make suggestions on how you want it changed."

"I haven't the time or patience to talk to the staff. That is your job."

Annabel could see that no matter what she said it was not getting through to him, so she left saying that she would see what could be done. She went to the restaurant to have a coffee and wait till a reasonable hour to telephone the PR company and speak to the managing director. Something had to be done or she would lose all the good staff that she had.

She was put through to the MD immediately, and although she didn't want to cause trouble for Jeffery, she had to explain that he was being unreasonable in his demands.

"I am so sorry to bother you, but Jeffery has insisted on changing the way we work and has demanded that we sack everyone and re-employ new people for no real reason that I can fathom. We have done this with only a few hours' notice, which is not possible.

"The directive seems to be changing from what we had been asked to do and I need a clear understanding of who we should take instructions from. We will of course do whatever you want, I just need to be told."

"I am sorry Annabel that you are having these problems as we are hearing only good things about the promotion and the newspaper is very pleased with how things are going. Leave it with me and I will speak to Jeffery and come back to you later in the day."

Annabel booked herself into a room and took the opportunity of taking a few hours' sleep until she was woken by Gemma knocking at her door.

"Mum, whatever you said worked as Jeffery has left and gone back to London and everyone is so happy. You have worked your magic, so thank you. When you are up can you phone the Birmingham team, there was a problem that I think you need to hear about. Don't worry it has been sorted but a phone call would not go amiss."

Annabel called the manager and he told her what had occurred.

"We set up a room at the depot for people to come in and sign up and we were really busy but I could see that there was a lot of disruption outside, so I went to investigate. There was a gang of young, rough-looking youths harassing the people who were waiting to sign up and telling them not to come in as we had enough staff. When I went over to the young boy who looked like the leader, I told him to move away and he pulled back his jacket to show me that he was carrying a gun.

"'Look mate I don't want any trouble but I am here to tell you that you can only use my crew or you will be hurt and so will anyone who tries to take the work away from us,' he said

"One of my team had seen what was happening and had called the police and within moments three police cars arrived, and the boys scarpered. We are always now having security men on duty, so I don't think we will have any more trouble."

Annabel was aghast at this story and asked if he would arrange to serve coffee and cakes that day for anyone who signed up in case word got around and frightened people off, and to thank everyone for the way the incident was handled. She told the manager that drinks that evening were on her for the team.

She also received a call from the PR company saying that Jeffery was under a lot of strain and he had been recalled to London and to please just carry on as she had been doing. No real apology but a good result, nevertheless.

At the end of the week Gemma and Annabel took the train back to London with the rest of the team and while Gemma was chatting to them and talking about the promotion Annabel could see a woman in their carriage who had been listening intently to the conversation get up and approach Gemma

"Sorry to interrupt you but I have been listening to you and your work sounds very interesting. I love the way you describe everything. I am from a TV company and we are at the moment looking to produce a reality TV programme and I would love to introduce you to the producer."

She handed Gemma a card and went back to her seat.

"Well Mum, you are not the only star of the family," said Gemma waving the card and laughing.

That was a great way to finish with laughter on what had been, a very fraught few days.

Chapter Forty
Simon

Poppy opened her nursery school in north London with her friend from the Montessori college and had asked Annabel to come and see it in operation. She had been able to take over the whole building and the girls had transformed the house into a nursery environment for small children.

Poppy had done her homework before opening and found a need for more nursery places in her area and had 35 children already enrolled but with a capacity to have 70 it looked like it could be very successful.

Both the girls' parents had helped with funds for the start-up and the photographs that Poppy had sent through looked amazing. There was an entrance hall with rows of small pegs leading to a large toilet block with cubicles and small sized toilets and sinks.

The main area was open-plan but had been divided up with shelving units so that the children could access different areas of learning and play, they also had a separate baby room, sleep room, staff area and kitchen.

Poppy had asked if Annabel could help with some of the administration as they couldn't really afford to pay anyone just yet. "It will only be simple things like keeping track of our invoices and making sure they are paid on time and if you could setup a spreadsheet with the children's details, we can probably manage to invoice the parents from our end."

Poppy had moved out of the flat she shared with her sister and had for the moment rented a place near to the nursery. She seemed to be working very long hours but had found the time to date a new boy that she had met. And by all accounts it seemed to be going well.

"Mum, when we next have a break can I bring him home so that you can meet him, he works in the city as a trader and has most weekends free. I would love for him to see our home in Portsmouth."

"Poppy you know your friends are always welcome just let me know when you both have a free date and I will try and arrange for the other children to join us. Simon has called me as he wants to come down this weekend as he said he has something he wants to tell me. Do you know what that is about?"

"No Mum, it is probably something to do with his course at uni."

....

Simon was expected any moment and Annabel was looking forward to seeing her youngest son as it had been many weeks since he had last been home.

The door was flung open as Simon came in carrying bags, which looked full of his clothes ready for washing. He dumped the black bin liners on the floor and grabbed Annabel in a giant hug.

"Hi Mum, it's good to see you, sorry about the washing I have got a little behind and I hope you have something for me to eat as I am so hungry."

"I am glad to see that nothing much has changed," laughed Annabel as she moved the bags to the utility room for later.

"I am making you a roast dinner for this evening but take a sandwich for now and I will make you a coffee or would you prefer a beer?"

"Anything will do, just so I can feed the inner man, you remember how much a growing lad like me needs to eat."

They sat companionly in the kitchen whilst Simon was eating. He didn't mention why he had come down this particular weekend or what he wanted to tell her, and Annabel didn't want to push him. He would tell her in his own time she thought.

Simon went up to his room when he had finished eating while Annabel attacked the mountain of washing that he had brought home. She knew that he would expect to go back to uni with some food supplies, so she looked through her cupboard to start to make up a box of things that he liked. She thought she would go out to the shops later to buy more, perhaps Simon would like to come with.

"Hey Simon," she called up to him, "I am going to the shops for some supplies for you, want to join me?"

"Ok, just give me a moment while I change, and I will be with you."

They shopped in the local supermarket and filled her car up with the shopping, it's a good thing that he brought his own transport with him thought Annabel, what with the washing and food he would need a truck to get back.

Later that evening after Simon had polished off most of the roast dinner she had cooked, Annabel thought that Simon had gone a little quiet and was looking flushed as he started to speak.

"Mum I have been wanting to tell you something for quite some time now but it never seemed the right moment, you know that I have been going out with Rachell for a while now. Well, I have started to see someone else and I thought that you should know."

"Darling you don't have to tell me who you date that is up to you. What's the name of your new girlfriend? I look forward to meeting her."

"You have already met, it's Ben," with that Simon burst into tears.

Annabel took her precious son in her arms and held him close to her until his tears had stopped.

"Ben is a very nice young man, and all that matters to me is that you are happy. I remember when you brought him down to meet us, he seemed very grounded and thinking about it you both make a great couple."

"Mum, you are taking this really well. I was so worried to tell you and the family. I kept putting it off, but Ben said that I should speak to you as he felt that you would understand."

"You should never be frightened to speak to me. You know that you can tell me anything and it never goes any further. Darling I don't hold the blueprint to your life, you make your own decisions of what you want to do and where you want to go, but just remember that wherever that is I am right by your side. Do you want me to tell Dad, Barry and the girls or is this something you want to tell them yourself? You know it won't make any difference to them; they all love you just as you are."

"Now that I have found the courage to speak to you, I think that I will tell them myself, but it would be good if you are there."

They discussed that Simon would wait until David was back on leave and then try and get all the children at home so that he wouldn't have to go through the trauma of telling them separately.

It was such a lovely, few days they spent on their own as Simon was able to talk to Annabel and tell her about his relationship with Ben, and how he had come to the understanding that he was gay. He said that a few of his friends at uni knew but he didn't feel that it made any difference to their friendship. It was accepted just as it was if you were of a different colour or religion and he felt comfortable with them.

After Simon had loaded his car with everything and given Annabel a massive hug before he drove back to London she sat on her own thinking about her family and how proud she was of them all. They all had achieved success in their chosen fields even if there had been some rough patches on the way, and they had made a life for themselves on their own terms.

Barry was working for himself now selling property and had met a wonderful girl that he was now living with and she expected that soon they might hear wedding bells. Poppy was happy with her nursery and her new man, even Gemma had seemed to have settled down and was such a real help in the agency, bringing in work through the contacts she made but with Gemma you could only hold your breath until the next moment that some new disaster faced her. And now her baby Simon, what courage he had had to tell her about his new relationship.

The only problem was with her husband David, as they were not communicating very much and had seemed to be drifting apart as even when he was at home, he was always out pursuing his own pleasures and was spending much of his time on his boat with his own friends which didn't seem to include her. They really must find time to sit down and discuss this and find out how they could mend the hole that seemed to have grown in their marriage and what they must do to repair it.

Maybe the problem was her, as she had Shawn now who had taken up much of the space in her heart, and perhaps there was not enough room for David. She had read somewhere that you can love two people at one time so she must try to understand where she and David had gone wrong and put it right.

Chapter Forty-One
Freddie

Walking into the London office Annabel could hear crying. Who on earth was that? she thought as she opened the door. In a corner of the office she could see Freddie with his head on the desk. Great sobs were coming from him and a box of tissues was by his hand.

"Freddie my darling boy, what on earth is the matter?" "Annabel, I have just heard that my best friend is in hospital, he is so ill, and they have told him that he might not have long to live. We all knew that he was HIV positive, but he was doing so well. This has come as a great shock. We should have noticed that he was losing so much weight, but he now has developed pneumonia." Freddie put his head into his hands again as if it was just too much trouble to breathe or speak.

Annabel took Freddie in her arms to hold him until he could stop crying and talk.

"Freddie how can I help you? Do you want to go to the hospital now? If you do, just leave and don't worry we will be able to manage. Gemma is due in shortly and she can cope, I want you to just focus on your friend nothing else is important."

"Yes please, Annabel, I need to go and see him. This might be the last time and I need to say goodbye." Freddie burst into tears again. Annabel held him close. She couldn't bear to see him in such agony, she knew how close he was to his friend. When he seemed to have got hold of himself and the sobs had diminished, she handed him his jacket and put it round his shoulders and gave him some money so that he could take a taxi and pushed him out of the door.

She was so sorry to hear about this as she had met the boy and to hear that he might not survive was devastating news but she had to quickly put into action some backup plans in case Freddie was unable to return to work in the near future. The south coast office was coping well with the newspaper promotion and they could, if needed, take on the calls for work that came through to London by transferring them. She had an immediate problem as she had to attend a final meeting that day at Heathrow Airport, and she had to leave just as soon as Gemma arrived.

Heathrow wanted to run fashion shows for their fashion shops in Terminal 2 and Annabel had been given the contract. It involved much work to organise passes airside for all the staff, as they had to provide all sorts of ID before the passes were issued. Lesley was organising this and had everything in hand. Gemma was styling the shows and all the dancers and promotional staff had been booked, it just needed a final briefing which she was on her way to attend.

She tried to make a call through to Freddie to make sure that he had arrived at the hospital but his phone was switched off so she would try and catch up with him later in the day.

While she was waiting for Gemma to arrive, she called the south coast office so she could tell Lesley what had happened to Freddie's friend.

"Annabel I am glad you called. I have found some discrepancies with the number of staff we are supplying for the newspaper promotion and the number of payments that we are making each week."

"Lesley what do you mean? Are we missing some payments, as you know we have employed a whole team of bookkeepers to run the payroll each week and if staff are not being paid, I need to find out what is happening."

"No, the problem is not that we are missing payments but when I did a check, I found that we are paying far more people than the numbers of staff we employ."

Annabel took a moment to digest what Lesley was telling her. It sounded like fraud, but who could be fraudulently claiming for payments and how were they doing it?

"Annabel until we look into this thoroughly I do not want to accuse anyone but the only way this could have been happening is from the payroll team, as when I send through the numbers of staff and hours worked it has been thoroughly checked by our team; it could be possible to add extra people on to the list at this stage. Can I suggest that we ask the head bookkeeper to come in and show us the payments that she has recorded? We will tell her that your accountant has requested this."

"Yes, Lesley please set this up. We need to get to the bottom of this immediately before it gets any more serious. Can you check the figures and let me know what happens when you meet with the bookkeeper? We have to be very careful before we accuse them, and we would have to have evidence to prove our findings but thank you for letting me know."

Gemma had come in by then and heard about Freddie and as she didn't have any meetings that day would stay in the office.

"Don't worry Mum. If I have to go out, I will transfer the calls to the south coast. I will also try and speak to Freddie; he must be in bits."

Annabel was driving to her appointment, but her head was full of the news about the poor boy who was in hospital, really nothing was important except your health she thought. But now she should concentrate on the meeting as the shows started in two days and as they were only given permission to rig the stage and set from midnight, they could only start the dress run in the early hours of the morning. What a fun way to work.

....

The stage and set with video wall were nearly completed and she needed to get back to the hotel for a few hours' sleep before the dress rehearsal which was due to start at 5 a.m. when all the dancers arrived.

Gemma had left the airport an hour before but had phoned through to Annabel with the number of the room they were sharing.

A very weary Annabel was dragging her case across the car park as there was no one to help her at this time of night and as it was only a Travel Lodge it was very basic.

There was no one at reception to ask which floor she was on, so she checked the room number she had written down and took the lift to the second floor. just her luck she thought that the room was the furthest one from the lift.

Arriving at last at the room, she knocked very lightly on the door, but no answer, so she knocked much harder, still no one came. This is ridiculous thought Annabel as she banged on the door. "Open up, I need to sleep. Come on Gemma this is not funny, open the fucking door NOW."

There was movement from inside the room at last and the door was opened by a very large man completely in the nude, and very angry.

"What the hell are you doing at this ungodly hour? What do you want?"

"Oh, I am so sorry I must have got the wrong room number," said Annabel stepping back. She grabbed her case and with as much strength as she could manage dragged it behind her as she made her way to the lift again. When she was out of sight of the nude man, she took out her phone and called Gemma

"Gemma what number room are you in I have just woken up a very angry man," Gemma repeated the room number which when Annabel checked was what she had written down

"Are you sure"

"Mum, of course I am sure I am sitting up in bed waiting for you and have even made you a cup of tea. Where the hell are you?"

Annabel had a horrible feeling so there was silence before she asked what the name of the hotel was, they were staying at. When Gemma told her, she started to laugh. She had not only knocked on the wrong room but in the wrong hotel.

Dragging her case back to the car park she couldn't stop laughing. What a stupid woman she was, how had she got that so wrong?

The next morning on site at the dress rehearsal after Gemma had promised that no one would hear about the night before, she had said that she might need a very nice gift to help her forget. Despite the promises everyone soon knew, and

Annabel was subjected to much teasing.

Annabel had spoken to Freddie who was very upset as his friend had died and he was organising his funeral and arranging to have all their friends together afterwards so that they could celebrate his life.

"Annabel I am so sorry but at the moment I have too much to do and I am not in a very good frame of mind to work. I thought that after the funeral I would go to visit my mother who lives up north, as I really feel like I need some quiet time with not a lot to think about."

"Freddie you must take all the time you want. There is no pressure to come back, why don't we say that for the next two months you are on leave. I will of course pay you and after that time let's talk and see how you feel. It might be that I transfer the business completely to the south coast and if that is the case you can come and work for me there. You know we feel that you are like one of the family so whatever you decide is OK with me."

Annabel hung up the call feeling depressed, so much seemed to be changing in her life. She needed to make some decisions. She had opened her office in London because she needed to make a name for the agency but now, many years later, she could be anywhere in the country as she had built a name for herself and clients were calling her when they needed a show or promotion; so the need for a London base had gone away.

The one good thing in her life was that her children all thriving and living good lives; or so she thought.

Chapter Forty-Two
Drugs

She was woken up by the telephone ringing. At first, she thought that she was dreaming as when she looked at the clock it was only 6 a.m.

"Hello, who is this?"

"This is a friend of Gemma's I thought that you should know that she has been using drugs and needs your help." Then the phone went dead in Annabel's hand. She looked at the handset with amazement. What was that about? She tried to call the number back, but it was withheld so she placed a call through to Gemma. It rang several times before Gemma answered.

"Gemma this is Mum, are you OK? I have just had a strange call from someone who didn't leave his name but said you are on drugs and needed me."

"Mum why are you calling me so early? Just ignore that call. It is someone playing around. I am fine. Speak to me later when I am awake," and she hung up.

Annabel could not get back to sleep after that, she was worried. It was a very cruel thing to have done by making a prank call, but thinking about it Gemma did not sound her usual chirpy self but it was 6am.

Annabel got up and had a bath and got dressed before she felt it was a reasonable time to call Gemma again. This time all she got for her trouble was a mouthful of abuse, which wasn't like her daughter at all.

"Mum leave me alone; you are always on my case. What do you think I am doing shooting up heroin? So, I take a reefer now and again, so what?" and she hung up.

This time Annabel could not settle but did not know who she could speak to but decided to wait until later when Gemma would be at the office and perhaps then she could find out what was going on.

It was late when Gemma finally arrived not looking very happy and unwilling to talk. Annabel locked the office door and put all the telephones on to answer and asked Gemma to sit down.

"OK, Gemma I think it is time we had a serious talk. Something is obviously wrong, I don't know if it is drugs or something else, but you must tell me what is going on."

Gemma was looking down at the floor as if deciding if she could talk. She was flushed, and her hands were shaking as she looked up.

"Mum, I don't suppose you will want to hear this but yes I have been taking drugs, and I realised a while ago that I needed some help with my addiction so I contacted a help centre and they told me to go to a day centre for help with drug addiction in Notting Hill. I have been going there for the past two months, that is where I have been when you cannot get hold of me."

"Gemma why didn't you tell me this before? I am pleased to hear that you want help now but tell me what I can do for you?"

"Mum I don't know. I don't feel that the centre is the right place for me, there are so many addicts there and only a few people who give advice. I think it would be better if I could go to a rehab where I could concentrate on getting better."

Annabel was so shocked at this news and felt rather out of her depth, but she had to find out about the best care she could. Perhaps the best way to start was to phone her doctor and ask him for advice but first she needed to close the office for the day and take Gemma back with her to the apartment so she could make calls in relative peace.

She spent the rest of the morning on the telephone calling the places that her doctor recommended. She had made Gemma lay down as by this time she was crying and quite out of control and her first priority was to ensure that Gemma was well looked after and in a safe place.

Eventually she was put through to a residential rehabilitation centre in Canterbury and spoke to the manager who advised her that first she needed a referral from her doctor and once that had been obtained Gemma would have a short-stay rehabilitative programme of 12 weeks at the centre to have a complete break from her current circumstances. Staying at a centre would mean that she would be away from their home and drug-using environment.

An appointment was made for that afternoon at the doctors so that she could be referred quickly.

Annabel insisted that Gemma stay with her until confirmation was received that a place was available for her in Canterbury. The funding for the rehab was from social services and Gemma would be given a social worker whom she had to report to.

The next two days were very stressful as Gemma found it very hard to settle and spent most of the night pacing the floor which was obviously a sign of her need for drugs but soon all was in place and they were on their way to Canterbury.

When they arrived, they were shown into an office and met with one of the counsellors who explained what would happen over the next three months.

"You will be allocated a keyworker who will agree a clear care plan with you, which will be reviewed in one-to-one keywork sessions. The care plan will set out your goals for treatment and include information about the aftercare that will be available when you finish the programme. There will also be a discussion about what will happen if you leave in an unplanned way.

"Gemma you will also be expected to participate in regular group-work sessions with other residents, and a range of tasks around the house; domestic duties or gardening, for example and you will be able to, when we feel you are ready, access leisure facilities either on or off-site."

Gemma was listening intently but did not ask any questions, but Annabel wanted to know how often she could visit.

"I am sorry but there are no visits for at least two months but Gemma will be able to call you a little later in the programme, and when we feel she is ready you will be invited to join her at a family group session."

Gemma and Annabel hugged each other when it was time for Annabel to leave.

"I can't begin to know what drove you to start using but understand that I am proud of the way you have recognised the need for help, and I am here for you every step of the way."

"Mum please don't tell Dad or the others. just say I am away working."

"Whatever you want. I love you Gemma and together with

the help you are receiving you will beat this."

Annabel had only spoken to Gemma a couple of times since she had been at the rehab centre but had now been invited to take part in a group family session and was not sure what that involved.

"Thank you all for coming here today but first I must ask you to please remember that anything that is spoken about is confidential and must not be discussed outside this room. I want to ask you please to state your first name and the name of your family member you are here to support. I will then go around the room for at least part of the session, to hear everyone's view of the problem that brought you to treatment."

The session was relaxed, and it was helpful to hear that Annabel was not alone and other families were also in the same situation and to hear how they were coping.

Gemma showed Annabel over the house where she was staying and the bedroom she was sharing with two other girls, which was quite basic with a bed, wardrobe and a bedside table.

Gemma told her a story about one of the girls who had like all of them to give a urine sample each day to make sure they were clean and as she had a joint the night before she knew she would not pass, so had asked Gemma to please provide the sample which she had then put into a condom and stored it in the fridge. The next morning, she put the condom in a glass of boiling water to warm it up before being asked to go into the toilet and provide a sample which she poured into the sample jar. Annabel thought that this was ingenious but stupid and hoped the story was about another girl and not Gemma who had had the joint, she wasn't sure at that moment if she could trust all that Gemma told her.

Before Annabel left, she was asked to come to a meeting with the counsellor.

"Annabel, I think that Gemma will benefit from an extended stay at a centre but unfortunately we will not be able to have her stay here as we are full up. I have arranged for her to go to a very good centre in Northampton and will make arrangements so she can be transferred there."

With the restrictions on not visiting and the distance from home it was unlikely that Annabel could see Gemma very much but anything that could help in Gemma's recovery had to be done.

Annabel found it very difficult not to be able to talk to anyone about Gemma and her addiction to drugs but she had promised Gemma and didn't like to break her promise but she needed some support herself so decided to speak to Shawn. Just speaking about how she was feeling would help.

Shawn was very supportive and said that he would speak to some colleagues of his to see if there was anything else that could be done.

"Annabel you will get through this and so will Gemma but I think that you perhaps need to tell your husband, keeping this from him is really not a good idea, he would want to help his daughter as much as he can."

Annabel felt much better for having shared her worries with Shawn but although she understood that she should tell David she thought that there was nothing that he could do at this moment so she would wait until he was home and she could tell him face to face.

After a month Annabel received a call from Northampton that Gemma had been asked to leave as she had been found sharing a bed with another resident; he too was asked to leave.

When she spoke to Gemma, she had told her that the home was full of very rough people. She was the only female there and had been verbally abused by another resident. She felt very uncomfortable which she realised was no excuse for sleeping with someone which was strictly against the rules.

"Mum can you send me money for the train ticket and for my friend as he also needs to get home."

"Gemma, that is not going to happen. I will drive up and collect you and although I am sorry about your friend, he will have to ask his own family to help him."

"Mum don't you trust me? What do you think I will do with the money? You really are a bitch sometimes," and with that Gemma hung up.

After collecting Gemma from the house in Northampton they had a very uncomfortable drive home as Gemma did not talk to her but sat with her arms crossed looking out the window.

Annabel couldn't keep Gemma a prisoner but didn't trust her to be on her own as she might try and score some drugs and then she would be back where she started.

Enough of this thought Annabel she had to take matters in her own hands. She didn't think any more funding would be available for the recovery, but it sounded like Gemma still needed all the help she could get so after some research she found that The Priory was undoubtedly the very best residential rehabilitation centre and there was a facility in London, so she called and made an appointment to see them as she needed to ask how much the treatment would cost and exactly how they could help her.

The house was in Roehampton and must have been at one

time a very luxurious private residence set in beautiful grounds, with a very grand entrance hall and furnishings.

She was shown up to the office and explained the treatment that Gemma had been given to date but said she wanted her to come to The Priory as long as she could afford the fees. If not, she needed to take out a loan if she could not pay for it herself. The manager of the facility was so nice and helpful and assured Annabel that they could help. After they mentioned the fees and saw the shock on Annabel's face, they asked what she could afford, which was just a fraction of the real cost.

"Don't worry Annabel we are here to help so we will accept that amount and your daughter can stay here until we are happy that she is well on the road to recovery. We will ask that you attend all the sessions for family members as that is important and you will need to meet with her counsellor weekly so that they can discuss with you the treatment she is receiving."

"I cannot begin to thank you for your help, and your understanding, I will of course be available whenever you ask. I am fully committed to your programme and will do everything I can to help my daughter."

Annabel was crying as she left The Priory, there were such good people in the world, although The Priory was a business, they had agreed to treat Gemma regardless that she could not pay the full amount.

The next few months would be hard for both of them, but Annabel felt confident that she had at last found the right place for Gemma to be and now she must find the strength to speak to her friends and tell them what was going on in her life and with their support she could get through this.

Chapter Forty-Three
Ireland

Gemma was doing well, and her counsellors were pleased at her daily sessions so Annabel felt that she could take a little time for herself. She had been invited by Shawn to join him for a few days away in Ireland. She was at first reluctant to leave in case she was needed but he had persuaded her that looking after herself was just as important as all she was doing for Gemma.

"I need to meet with my solicitor in Dublin and when I have finished, I thought that I could show you some of the beautiful parts of the country that I fell in love with. There is an amazing hotel about 60 miles from Dublin in the foothills of the Slieve Bloom mountains in County Laois. I promise you that you will never have experienced the five-star luxury that you will find at this country house hotel. It is a place of history, luxury, romance and tranquillity which is just what you need and deserve at this moment."

"You have convinced me, in fact there is not much that you can't persuade me to do, but I do like the sound of luxury, romance and tranquillity and as long as that is on the menu, I am ready."

Shawn had booked flights for them from Gatwick early on Friday morning so that he could meet with his solicitor. He told Annabel that while he was at his meeting, she could have the chance of doing some shopping, as he knew how much she loved this pastime.

Shawn had told her that Grafton Street was one of the most beautiful shopping streets in the world and she could see why it had been given that description. There were so many shops and boutiques and an abundance of restaurants and live music was playing on nearly every street corner. She was on a mission to find some gifts for Shawn and at the first boutique she came to she saw the most beautiful sweaters in the window so pushed open the door to have a look round.

She purchased two cashmere sweaters from one of Ireland's trendiest designers and a couple of silk ties that she thought would go very well with his business suits. She asked for them to be gift wrapped and left with satisfaction of having found the perfect gifts. It was early so she wandered along the street at a leisurely pace stopping at a café and sitting in the sunshine so she could hear the music from a street musician.

By early afternoon Shawn had telephoned to say he had finished with his meeting and arranged to collect her at the entrance of St Stephens Green. They took a slow drive through the country before arriving at the hotel that Shawn had booked for them.

The countryside was breath-taking, and the beauty of the landscape was something that she would always remember. They stopped at a famous inn for a pint of Guinness before heading onto the hotel which sat at the foot of the Slieve Bloom Mountains.

They pulled up to the front of the hotel and were immediately greeted by the doorman who welcomed them. The hotel was truly magnificent and on entering Annabel looked around at the wonderful works of art and antiques before being shown up to their suite where they were to stay for two nights.

A magnificent canopied bed stood in the middle of the room dressed in heavy white drapes; there was antique furniture around the room and the walls were covered in blue silk and adorned with paintings and mirrors and from the ceiling hung a large chandelier. There were two bathrooms one of which had the biggest bath Annabel had ever seen. From the bedroom were double doors leading to a balcony which was not overlooked so they have their breakfast out there in complete privacy. It was just amazing and as soon as the cases were delivered, and the door closed Annabel threw herself into Shawn's arms and with a cry of delight hugged him tight.

"Oh, thank you. this is heaven."

"I am so pleased you like my choice. You deserve the best. What would you like to do first?" said Shawn as Annabel made very clear what she wanted to do as she was undressing him as she planted kisses onto his face and trying to get out of her own clothes at the same time which dropped onto the floor in a heap.

They fell together onto the floor laughing as she climbed on top of Shawn and without any prelude pushed his cock inside her; she didn't need any assistance to get ready she was wet just from being close to him and Shawn was more than ready as he was rock hard. They both needed to feel each other and wanted to be as close together as two people could be.

Shawn pulled out a little way before plunging hard into her, again and again and Annabel could feel his thrusts reaching even further each time until she thought that she couldn't take any more of him, she could feel her insides start to pulsate with each thrust and a hot feeling travelled all over her body and a wonderful feeling in her stomach which felt like waves breaking until in a rush she came with a loud cry of release. Shawn on hearing her cry out pushed for one more time and he climaxed just seconds behind her.

"Yes," he said, "that is exactly what I wanted to do."

They lay for a while on the soft carpet as they were too spent to move until Annabel suggested that they try the bath before getting ready to go down for dinner.

They had a warm bath in scented bath oils where they washed each other until Shawn insisted that Annabel get out of the bath and get ready for dinner as he had a surprise for her.

Annabel dried her hair and put on fresh makeup as there was not much left as Shawn had kissed most of it away and she dressed in a stunning new evening dress she had bought especially for this evening. She put on new silk stockings as Shawn liked them better than tights and her new high heels shoes and she was ready.

When she came into the lounge, she saw Shawn sitting in an armchair by a small table which held a bottle of Champagne in a bucket and a large vase of red roses.

"Are those for me?"

"Yes, my darling girl, they are for you."

She went forward to smell them and saw that there was a small box next to them. She looked at Shawn and he just smiled and handed her the box which she opened. Inside was the most exquisite diamond bracelet, a bracelet that she could wear every day as it was so elegant and so beautiful. She was speechless as he looked at him.

"Why do you spoil me so much. Just being here with you is all that I need."

"I want you to know how much you mean to me, and I enjoy giving you gifts, it pleases me to know that you will wear it and think of me."

"Shawn, I do not know how to thank you. You are so very special to me," she stepped forward to kiss him when she remembered that she had bought him some gifts earlier in the day and had not as yet given them to him.

She went to the wardrobe and brought out the bags which she handed to him. "I am sorry, but they are not quite as beautiful as your bracelet, but I hope you like them."

Shawn was delighted with his gifts and told Annabel that he seldom received anything to wear as all his gifts seemed to be things he could use in his office.

They went down to the restaurant and were seated at a small table with candles and flowers, the whole setting was magnificent. They chose the tasting menu which had been recommended and it was superb. Annabel kept sneaking looks at her bracelet and smiling when she saw Shawn watching her.

They were both sated with food and wine and their early love making so when they went to bed, they didn't feel the need to do anything but kiss and hold each other close until they fell asleep.

Annabel was woken with a delicious feeling throughout her body as if tiny little birds were flapping their wings above her and the breeze was cooling her until she realised that Shawn was blowing kisses to see if she was awake.

"Hey there, sleepy head, I have been watching you sleeping and I have to tell you that you are as beautiful asleep as you are awake." Then he began to caress her body with his fingers, starting at her face and then down her neck, he stopped to plant small bites on her ear lobes and then down to her breasts were he rubbed them taking her nipples between his fingers until they became hard and firm, and then down her belly until he reached her vagina where he explored her, running his fingers inside until he could feel her starting to get wet. He moved his body until his face was between her legs and with his tongue pushed it inside and moving it round, he could see that Annabel was enjoying this as she was making little sounds at the back of her throat. She arched her back and pushed hard against his mouth until he could feel her juices running down.

"Now Shawn it's my turn." She moved herself on top of him and with her mouth put it over his cock and slowly moved her tongue round him then put her lips on the tip and sucked, slowly at first and then taking all of him into her mouth until he came with a grunt.

"What a beautiful way to wake up. Shall I order breakfast and then we can go out for a walk or if you prefer, I can arrange a boat for the lake, and I can order a picnic for our lunch."

"That sounds like a perfect way to spend the day," said Annabel as she got up and made her way into the bathroom. She emerged a while later to see that breakfast had been served on the balcony and Shawn was already sitting out there drinking a cup of coffee and what delighted Annabel was that he was wearing one of his new sweaters.

They spent a leisurely day on the lake and had the picnic lunch that had been prepared for them by the hotel. That night they dined again in the restaurant this time with a simpler fare.

That night's love making was as every bit as good as ever with each of them giving pleasure to the other, with gentle caresses and kissing.

Annabel thought that this weekend had been so perfect she was so sorry to leave and go back to the reality of her life. Saying goodbye to Shawn was the hardest thing of all.

Chapter Forty-Four
Fraud

The weekend had given Annabel the strength and the resolve to speak to David about the situation with Gemma as keeping him in the dark was not good and he would be upset that he had not been told.

She put a call to the base and asked if a message could be given to her husband as there was a family emergency that she needed to talk to him about.

A few hours later David was on the phone.

"Annabel, I received a message that you urgently needed to talk to me. What is the matter?"

The conversation was difficult, how do you explain that your daughter was on drugs and was now in a rehabilitation centre receiving treatment for her addiction, and that she had been staying at rehab centres for quite some time.

"David I am so sorry but with you so far away I didn't think that you could give any practical help and you would only spend your time worrying. She is now in the place she needs to be and receiving all the help she needs."

Annabel burst into tears; it was such a stressful situation she knew that she liked to cope on her own but sometimes you had to reach out to someone else to share the burden.

"Annabel do you want me to come home?"

"No David there is nothing either of us can do at this

moment and you would not be able to see her, but I am sure that if I speak to the Priory, they can arrange for you to speak to Gemma yourself which I am sure would be good for both of you."

"Yes, please arrange this and let me know when I can speak her. Annabel why do you always take things onto your own back? You keep things hidden from me which I don't like. When I am next back home, we both need to have a talk, I need to know what is going on at home at all times and not be kept in the dark, I can't believe that you have kept this a secret for all this time."

"David you are quite right I should have told you as soon as I heard and I am sorry but it was not to keep things hidden but when you are so far away, I thought that I could deal with this on my own and not worry you. But I realise that you need to be told and I need your support."

David was so angry both about Gemma and that Annabel had not spoken to him, she could hear it in his voice. He was upset and did not like it when his children were not the perfect people that he expected.

Annabel felt a little better after she had spoken with David and was only sorry she had not told him before. She would arrange with The Priory for David to speak to Gemma. But most importantly she now had to tell Gemma that her father knew, which properly wouldn't go down well with her, but Gemma seemed to be in a better place since being under the care of this rehab centre. The last time that she had visited during the family session Gemma had turned to her in front of everyone and said how sorry she was for messing up and asked to be forgiven. She had even got up from her chair and gone over to Annabel to give her a cuddle.

She was in the south coast office for a few days and would take this opportunity of finding out how the newspaper promotion was going and if they now had evidence of fraud with the staff payments.

Lesley the office administrator was now convinced that more people were being put onto the payroll system than had actually worked.

"I checked very thoroughly the list that was given to me by the payroll manager and there were names and addresses from local people that were definitely not working in the Midlands. How she thought that they get away with this I do not know."

"Lesley please arrange a new firm to take on the payroll, check with our accountant perhaps this is something he might be able to help with. Could you also give me a list of any names you think should not be there and the amounts that have been paid to them so I will take this off the final payment I owe to the bookkeepers. I will arrange to get the manager to come into see me this afternoon so that I can tell her face to face why she and her team are being sacked."

A very unpleasant half hour meeting took place and the conversation was difficult, but she had hard evidence that someone or a group of people were falsifying names. The head of the bookkeeping firm came in to see her and Annabel could see that she was unaware of why she had been called to this meeting. She was showed the list of names of staff who lived locally but were on the pay roll for work done in the Midlands and north of the country.

"Perhaps you have an explanation for this, and I am happy to listen but from what I can see someone has committed a serious crime."

After much bluster and denials of any wrongdoing Annabel had had enough.

"I want you to bring round to me immediately all the paperwork relating to this promotion and let me have a final bill from which I will deduct all the overpayments, which of course you can challenge in court, if it comes to that. I will have to report this to the police. Do not give my name as a reference to anyone as I would have to tell the truth and if I hear that you are still working as a bookkeeper, I will report you. Do you understand?"

The furious woman stormed out of the office banging doors as she went, she obviously knew that she had been found out and by paying her friends and family had been committing fraud.

The people Annabel had in the south coast office were working out very well and were a very good team. Lesley was very efficient and kept the office going together the other two staff who booked the models and promotional staff and did the paperwork that was needed. Lindy had also come in to work when they needed extra help as she now had had her baby but did not want to leave her to take up choreography again but liked being involved so was happy to work for the moment on a part-time basis and as she knew most of the people on the agency's books it was very helpful.

Annabel wondered if now was right time to close the London office as Freddie was still up north living with his mother as he had taken the death of his friend very hard. She couldn't see him returning to live and work again in London anytime soon.

She had a temporary booker running things in London as most of the important phone calls and messages were coming through to the south coast. She thought that she would wait a couple more months until the lease on the office came up for renewal before she made her final decision and she could always use the apartment for any meetings if she closed the office.

She needed now to concentrate on Gemma's recovery and to see if her marriage to David could survive this latest disaster.

Chapter Forty-Five
David

David was home again on leave, but he seemed to be avoiding Annabel and she could not pin him down so that they could talk. He was off today on his boat where he seemed to spend much of his time. Annabel had said she would go with him, but he told her that he preferred to be alone and as he only wanted to wash the boat down and do some minor repairs, there was nothing she could help him with.

They had arranged to have some friends over for a meal that evening so Annabel was busy in the kitchen preparing the main course which was ready to be put in the oven. She loved entertaining and rarely had the opportunity; not only the cooking but she spent as much time making the table look pretty.

There were going to be eight for dinner and she laid the table with a white linen tablecloth and made sure that all the correct cutlery was out with their best crystal wine and water glasses. She had put two small flower arrangements in the middle with roses cut from their garden and white and pink serviettes to pick up the colour scheme. Two candlesticks with pink candles completed the table arrangement, she only hoped the meal was as good as the table looked.

Annabel thought that relaxing with their friends would put David in a good mood so that the rest of the weekend would go smoothly and they would be able to sit down and talk properly.

First to arrive was Edna and her husband John, it was great to see Edna again and she wanted to find out how her restaurant was going; John was in the police force and great company. Next was her dear friend Jennifer who had a large family she looked after and also helped her husband Harry when he needed some office work done at home as he was a lawyer and was always busy. They had used his services many times over the years and trusted his advice. Last as usual was Alan who was a fellow officer of David's; quite a boorish man who only liked the sound of his own voice and spent all his time telling everyone how much money his family had, how much land they owned and the wonderful holiday they had all taken. His wife was Carole who Annabel did not care for very much, as at most of the dinners they had attended she got very drunk and had to be escorted home, and there was something about her that Annabel did not trust.

The evening was very lively, and much wine was consumed, the meal went down very well, and Edna had even asked for the recipe which was a great compliment as she cooked at her own restaurant. Alan as usual had taken over the conversation telling everyone about what he had got up to and rarely asking about anyone's else's life.

Carole was for most part sitting quietly just staring at her plate, but you could see that with each glass that she consumed her face was getting more flushed and when she did begin speaking all her conversation was directed at the men. Annabel could see that she had started to flirt with David who was sitting beside her. She didn't mind; perhaps it would put David in a good frame of mind. The room went quiet as she said so loudly everyone could hear

"David you are so handsome, and you have such a great body, I know that Annabel doesn't treat you right, perhaps if you invite me onto your boat again, we could have some more fun. We had such a good time when I last visited you, didn't we? We should do it again"

There was complete silence at Carole's words with everyone not really knowing where to look. Alan got up from his chair and turned to Carole.

"Come on my dear I think that you have had enough to drink so I will take you home. Sorry Annabel and David for leaving early but thank you for a pleasant evening." He pulled Carole up and half carried her to the door amidst her cries of protest.

The rest of the evening was quite uncomfortable with no one mentioning what Carole had said. David, Annabel could see was getting very drunk himself so when the other guests got up to leave, she thought that perhaps it was time to say goodnight to everyone.

"Annabel don't take too much notice of Carole she does not know what she is saying when she gets like this," said Jennifer as she kissed her on the check before saying goodbye.

As Annabel closed the door, she thought that perhaps the evening had been a very bad idea after all and now she had to confront David,

"I don't want to talk to you, I am going to bed," said David as he pushed Annabel out of his way so violently that she stumbled against the table. He made his way unsteadily up the stairs hanging onto both the banisters and knocking against the wall when he couldn't keep his balance.

Annabel went into the kitchen to tidy everything away and

to put the dishwasher on as she hated to get up in the morning to dirty plates. And it gave her something to do and stopped her thinking about what she had heard. She didn't blame David for having an affair, she had done the same thing, but David had had an affair with a friend of theirs which was stupid especially someone who drank and couldn't be trusted to behave was unbelievable.

As she undressed, she saw a very large bruise start to appear on her hip where David had pushed her. She decided to sleep in one of the children's bedrooms and perhaps in the morning when David had sobered up they could talk.

The next morning Annabel was up early. She had not been able to sleep at all with everything going through her mind. David did not appear until midday when he entered the kitchen and went straight over to the coffee machine to make himself a drink.

"Can I make you some breakfast?" asked Annabel but David totally ignored her and went into the garden to drink his coffee and have a smoke. She stayed in the kitchen making herself busy waiting for him to come back indoors which he did after half an hour but went straight into the lounge and sat down. Annabel followed him and took a seat.

"David, we do have much to talk about, but first can you please tell me what Carole was talking about last night. It was very embarrassing for everyone who heard her drunken conversation."

David sat very still looking down at the floor and when he looked up, she could see the anguish written across his face. He took a moment before he answered.

"Annabel I am sorry that you had to hear about the stupid short relationship with Carole that I had. I am ashamed of myself for getting involved with someone so close to home, and while we are talking about relationships, she was not the first, but I promise you it was never with anyone that you knew."

Well it seemed that they were opening up to each other at last.

"David that really is not the most important thing at the moment, and if we are talking honestly, I also have been unfaithful, but I have felt cut out of your life as I see so little of you and when you are home you seem to be in another place. Not here with me and the children. I know that I was wrong not to have told you about Gemma and the drugs, but we speak so rarely and then you don't want to hear about things at home."

"I know that I have not been here for you, but you knew when we married that I would be away for much of the time. I asked you to come with me, but you chose to stay in England. I understood that you wanted to make a life for yourself and our children and when your agency took off you had another interest, so you are partly to blame."

Annabel was starting to cry; she had always loved David but was not 'in love' with him anymore. He had been her first real boyfriend, and she had gone straight from her mother's house to living with David, never having been able to fend for herself; perhaps that was part of the problem. David had always treated her like a child so that when she had to think for herself and had the means, she had rebelled.

"David what do we do now? Can we mend the broken pieces of our marriage? I want to try as we both have invested so much in this marriage just to give up on it would be a shame. We could both try much harder, I can give up my business if that is what you want."

Annabel could see that David was not really listening to her, and his face looked like a stone with no kindness or sympathy etched on it.

"David please speak to me. Can we try? Or do you want a divorce?"

"Annabel, we have grown apart over the last few years and I think it would be better if we, for the moment, were separated. I don't think we can pretend that this is working but let us leave with some dignity and perhaps in the future we can become friends as we have the children to consider and they are the most important parts of our lives.

"I will go and pack some things and go and stay at the officer's mess for the moment. All the practical things we need to talk about we can do later. I am sorry Annabel, but I don't love you and I don't want to be with you anymore. I want to be on my own and live my life as I want without having to worry about you."

Annabel was shocked to hear David's cruel words; in all the time she had been with him she had never treated him so badly or not shown him the respect that she thought he deserved. But he obviously did not feel the same way about her. Perhaps this would be better for both of them to live apart. She would have to tell the children as she was sure that David would take the coward's way out and leave her to break the news.

She had to stay strong and look after everyone, which was really all that she had been doing all her married life.

Chapter Forty-Six
Decisions

Annabel had heard from friends who had gone through a divorce that no matter what had been promised it always ended up in a very acrimonious situation. David was keeping his distance and would not talk to her on the phone but had resorted to only responding through his solicitor which was causing all sorts of problems. Annabel needed him to sit down to discuss what assets they needed to sell and what they personally wanted to keep.

The most hurtful part was their children as David had not taken the time to see them but just made phone calls and then spent much of the time telling them how it was all theirs mother's fault as he did not want to separate but that Annabel had told him to get out of the house and that she did not love him anymore.

Annabel did not respond to these accusations as it would not help. The children although adults needed to know that both their parents loved them. She had asked to see them so that she could try and explain what was going to happen. Gemma was so angry with her and a very nasty conversation had occurred the night before when they had spoken on the telephone as Gemma was still in rehab at the Priory

"Mum, I know it is all your fault. You are so selfish; you only think about yourself and never consider Dad. He told me what a bitch you have been to him and how you have been trying to push him out of our lives for such a long time now. I don't want to see or speak to you anymore so don't try and come to see me; I hate you for what you have done," with that Gemma banged the phone down.

Annabel had spoken to The Priory and told them what was happening, and they had advised that Annabel stay away for a short while until Gemma had calmed down. They would ask her counsellor to speak with her before she visited again.

Barry and Simon were both very supportive and told her that they would not take sides but were there for her whenever she needed them, probably they understood a little better as they both were in stable relationships, Barry now living with Lillian and Simon had his friend Ben. Poppy had been a little distant, but she had always been 'Daddy's Girl' and it would take time for her to adjust.

She had spoken to Shawn and told him about the breakup, and he had been so lovely to talk to and had given her some practical advice.

"Annabel I am so sorry to hear what you are going through it must be so hard for you to cope with but stay strong and you will get through it. Get yourself a good solicitor and listen to his advice, and if you need to talk to me if you are unsure of anything just ask."

"Shawn, it is so good to speak to you and I do miss seeing you, but I don't think it would be wise for us to meet at the moment. I do not want to cause you any problems and certainly I do not want to give David any ammunition that he can use against me."

"I get that but perhaps if we meet at your apartment, I am sure it would be OK, and I too need to see you. Please do not

258

feel under any pressure from me as I will be happy just to be able to talk to you, just not quite as happy as seeing you but you are going through enough at the moment and I don't want to add to it with unfair demands."

"Shawn you are the only sane thing in my life at this moment, and seeing you would be wonderful, so yes let's meet London"

They had arranged to meet the following week as she had an appointment to visit her solicitor to try and work out an amicable arrangement to dispose of their assets.

"Annabel I have heard from David's solicitor and he is asking for what I think are unfair demands, he wants half the proceeds of the house, his car and he also wants clear title to his boat and wants you to pay him a maintenance amount monthly as he says that you have a successful business so you should look after him."

Annabel sat stunned and took a moment to think before she replied.

"David has only contributed to the running of the home and never anything towards the children's schooling. I paid for half the boat and took on the finance for his car. What I am prepared to agree to is this; we will sell our home and after the divorce costs have been taken off will pay him half, the boat he can keep, also his car. I will not pay him anything for maintenance as he receives good pay and when he retires he will have both a pension from the Navy and he also has an excellent private pension which he took out many years ago from family money he had been left so I should in fact be asking for maintenance from him. I will not move on this and if he wants to go to court just remind him that any proceeds from the house will be used up in court fees so he will not get very much, and in that case, I will also receive half the value from his boat."

"I agree Annabel that what you are prepared to give him is very fair, but I will also tell him that this offer is only available for the next four weeks. After this time, it will be withdrawn so let's see how quickly they come back. I must say Annabel that I would not like to have met with you across a court room," he said smiling at her.

They shook hands as Annabel left his office feeling confident that she had retained a good man to fight on her behalf. There were other practical things that had to be sorted but they could wait until confirmation from David had been made on what he would accept, so for the moment she must concentrate on her agency and the work that was coming in and she had her meeting with Shawn to look forward to.

When she was at the London office, she found a letter from Lottie her landlord asking her to please arrange to see her as the lease was coming up for renewal and she wanted to know what Annabel wanted to do. She immediately went upstairs to see if Lottie was free to talk and found her watching a keep fit class as she no longer took the classes herself.

She told Lottie about her pending divorce and how her life was going to change over the next few months.

"My dear, it sounds like you have rather a lot on your plate at the moment. Perhaps as you have told me now is the time to move the running of your business down to the south coast, you can stay on a month to month basis until you can sort it all out. Please do not worry as I was thinking of selling the property at the end of the year as it is getting a little bit for much for me; so perhaps the time is right for me also."

Lottie was a dear lady and Annabel gave her a big hug;

she had now made the decision to move — perhaps not the best time in her life as she soon had to look for a new place to live as well, but so be it.

Now she had a more important appointment. To meet up with Shawn. She quickly shopped for some food as they would both be hungry later, only something light as she wasn't in the mood to cook a large meal.

Soon after Annabel arrived at the apartment the doorbell rang to announce the arrival of Shawn and after pushing the door entry, she went to her front door to greet him.

"Just promise me that we will not talk about my husband, all I want to hear is about you and to hold you close."

Shawn wrapped his arms around Annabel as he gave her a kiss and seemed to reluctant to let her go.

"Don't you think we would be more comfortable if we moved away from the door and went inside?" she asked taking his hand in hers as she led the way to the kitchen. Shawn had found the time to buy her some beautiful flowers, red roses, her favourite and she arranged them in a vase.

"Help yourself to a drink and we can go and sit in the lounge."

Annabel caressed his face with her fingers and gave him kisses as they sat close to each other on the settee.

"My darling girl, I haven't seen you in such a very long time I can't stop from wanting to touch you. Please can I see you all of you now without your clothes, so I can feel you with my hands. I want to run my fingers over your body; every part of you."

Annabel stood up and moved a little way from where Shawn was sitting. She took off her jacket and put it on the chair, then undid her skirt and it fell on the floor, next she undid her shirt slowly and took it off until she was only standing in her bra, pants and stockings. She undid her bra and pulled off her pants and stockings and moved close to where Shawn was so he could touch her.

He put his hands on her legs and run them up so he could feel if she was getting wet with desire. He moved his thumb inside her and rolled it round, he then stood and lifted her up and carried her into the bedroom and gently laid her on the bed.

He spent a while not touching just looking at her body and then started at the top of her face running his fingers slowly as he needed to commit to memory all of her. It was exciting just to see Shawn looking but not touching; she felt her desire build until he moved his hands, first down onto her body and over her shoulders, arms and stopping at her breasts so he could stroke them and take her nipples in his mouth which he sucked on until they became hard. He moved his hands down cupping her bottom in his strong hands and kneading them, when he came to her vagina, he moved his body so his face could breathe her in, and his mouth could taste her.

He ran his tongue inside feeling her respond and her juices running onto his mouth.

He moved away so that he could push his cock into her vagina, moving very slowly and then faster and harder; it seemed as if he wanted to devour all of her.

"Wait," said Annabel moving herself so that she was now on top of his body, she held his hands above his head and put her breasts close to his mouth and his cock firmly inside. With slow movements at first and then moving quickly she could see that Shawn was nearly ready and with a final push he exploded just as she reached her own climax.

They lay close together breathing deeply and she could feel her heart start to slow down. Facing each other they kissed without saying a word as they knew what each of them felt without any words.

"I just want you to know that you have made me whole again, just being with you and feeling your love for me Shawn, without you in my life I do not know what I would have done. Thank you for being here with me."

For that brief afternoon when she was able to forget all the shit in her life Annabel was completely happy- a brief wonderful moment in time.

Chapter Forty-Seven
Devastating News

The solicitor telephoned to say that David had accepted her terms and she had put the house on the market and within a very short time had received a reasonable offer which she was prepared to accept, so now she was looking for a new home for her with enough room for the children when they came home.

Annabel was meeting an estate agent that day as she was interested in the details of a penthouse apartment on the seafront in Southsea, that he had sent her.

They took the lift to the third floor and he opened the door to a large bright apartment. The moment that Annabel stepped inside she knew that this was the place for her. There were three bedrooms of a good size, one of which she would use as her office but with a bed settee for when extra guests came. The kitchen was small and needed refurbishing but could be extended by knocking a wall down and making the hall leading to it smaller, the apartment had a bathroom and separate shower room and toilet but the piece de resistance was the lounge and dining room which could be separated by the glass doors but was magnificent just opened up, with windows both front and back of the building. There was a door which led onto the penthouse roof which extended over the complete building and had a glass balustrade around it. In the middle of the area was a brick building which housed the water tank but had plenty of room for storage inside. Climbing plants covered the brick and many ceramic tubs planted with small conifers and an abundance of flowers were laid out over the whole roof terrace, there were also several loungers with upholstered seats.

Annabel could hardly catch her breath; it was exactly what she wanted, even more so as it had this wonderful garden that looked over the seafront. The price was a little steep, but she would have enough from the proceeds of the house sale with just enough left over to make the improvements that she needed so she had to negotiate very carefully.

"I am interested but the price is a little too high for me. Would the owners accept an offer?"

"I can only pass on your offer, but I must tell you that there is someone else who has looked over the apartment and is interested but they still have to sell their own house."

"Well the good thing with me is that I can move very quickly as I have already sold my house. I'm just waiting for the sale to be completed as we have already exchanged. Please tell them the price that I am willing to pay and ask that they come back to me by next week because if I cannot buy this, I must look for another place or I will be homeless."

Annabel was really excited but had to wait until the agent came back to her and she did not have any room for movement on the price as most of the work that had to be done was necessary to make. She had also allowed an amount for decoration and some new furniture as David wanted half of the furniture they had already, and she was happy to give it to him as it would be so nice to have some new things.

By that afternoon the agent came back and told her that

the owners could go down in price by a small amount, but they were holding out for as near to the asking price as possible. Annabel thought that she could go a little higher if they were willing for the extra money to include all the terrace garden pots and furniture, so she told the agent and asked that he please make the owners understand that the offer was a full and final one and she needed to hear within a few days if it was accepted.

This was as exciting as when she first opened her office in London so she just had to cross her fingers that she would be able to buy the wonderful apartment.

Next on her shopping list was to relocate the office and she needed a small space where the agency could be run from. As this was only to rent it wasn't so hard to find suitable premises, two or three rooms would be sufficient but must have parking for the staff.

Within a week she had found space for the office and had signed the lease but was still waiting to hear about the penthouse and wondered what was taking so long when her mobile phone rang, and the call was from the agent.

"Annabel sorry not to have been in touch before but the owners were away for a few days and have only just come back to me, but I am delighted to tell you that they have accepted your offer."

Annabel was ecstatic with the news and she quickly put through a call to Harry to ask him if he would handle the legal work for her.

"Annabel my dear, how are you doing? I am so sorry that you and David have parted but after the evening we spent at your home I am not really surprised. I would be delighted to handle your new acquisition and we can make it fall in line with the sale. Jennifer and I will look forward to visiting you in your new home in due course."

Annabel now wanted to tell Shawn her news and as she had not spoken to him lately, she put a call through to his mobile, but it went straight to voicemail, so she left a message. Often when Shawn was busy, he did not answer but always called back by the end of the day, so Annabel was surprised not to have heard from him that evening. She did not want to call again in case he was with friends so decided to wait until the next day.

The next morning, she telephoned but again it went to voicemail and the same thing happened each time she rung. Something was wrong. It was so unlike Shawn not to call her; she hoped that it was nothing to do with his family but she had no way of contacting him privately unless she called the consulting rooms in Harley Street which she decided to do if by tomorrow she had not heard from him.

She waited the next day in case he rang her but when she could not wait any more as the suspense was killing her, she called through.

"I am so sorry to trouble you," she said to the receptionist when her call was answered, "But I wonder if it is at all possible to speak to Mr. Shawn Conner"

"I am so sorry, but he is not here today, but I will leave a message on his desk and ask him to call you back."

There was nothing more Annabel could do but wait until Shawn called her which he did late that afternoon.

"Shawn are you OK? I have been so worried."

"Annabel I am sorry but there were some very important matters that I had to deal with. I would like to meet with you when you have the time as there is something that I need to tell you."

"Shawn you are worrying me even more now, can't you tell me on the phone?"

"No, I am sorry Annabel, but I would rather see you in person. When can we meet?"

Annabel could not settle to anything until she could see Shawn and speak to him, so arranged to come up to London that evening and meet up in Baker Street.

When Shawn arrived, he looked drawn and tired, so Annabel waited until he was ready to tell her what the problem was.

"Annabel, I have not been deliberately avoiding you, but I have been undergoing some tests these last few months and I had to have an MRI scan earlier this week, so I was waiting to hear the results."

Annabel moved over to sit by him as he knew in her heart that she would be told some devastating news and wanted to be close.

"Annabel, I have the onset of Multiple Sclerosis, there is no cure but there are some treatments that will help, but the prognosis is not good and my symptoms will get worse, so I have decided to give up my practice immediately and retire. I shall probably sell our home in England and go and live in Ireland."

Annabel could not quite take in all that Shawn was telling her. She knew very little about this disorder but to lose this man would be terrible

"Shawn, I want to take care of you, I will be with you whenever and wherever you want, nothing is important to me but you."

"Annabel, I knew how you would react, but I am 20 years

older than you, and you still have all your life ahead and looking after a sick old man is not what I want to happen. I need to remember you and our marvellous times together with fondness and love; not be embarrassed by seeing you help me to wash and dress and to do all those things that would have to be done. Please understand I do not want you waste your life on me. Help me now please by saying goodbye and letting me go with whatever dignity I still have left."

Annabel could feel the tears running down her face, she couldn't stop them, her whole body was shaking but she knew this was not what Shawn wanted from her, she had to be strong for both of them. She wrapped her arms round his body and held him close to her heart.

She was so lucky to have had this man in her life but now she must do as he wanted and let him go, that would be the kindest thing for them both, not a drawn-out lingering time when his disorder would make him, in his eyes, less of a man.

"Shawn can you stay a while? Must you leave now? I need to hold you and give you memories that will make you smile when you think of me."

"Everything about you makes me smile and my memories are happy, joyous ones of every moment we have spent together, but I can stay here with you tonight if you will have me."

They went together to the bedroom and Annabel helped Shawn undress before she took off her own clothes. Tonight, was totally about him and giving him pleasure in whatever way she could.

She kissed him on his mouth putting her tongue inside and then kissed every part of his body, starting with his head his eyes his ears, she needed to feel and taste him, she trailed her lips down his chest until she came to his cock which she took into her mouth and with slow movements she run her tongue round him and sucked until she could feel him harden, moving her mouth away so she could watch him enjoy what she was doing. His eyes closed and his hands went into her hair and then pulled her head down until her mouth engulfed him and he came in a shuddering cry.

They lay holding each other all night as they knew it would be the very last time. Annabel couldn't take her eyes off him until sleep overcame her and she drifted away only half aware of where she was.

When she opened her eyes, it was morning and she felt cold, she was alone in her bed. Shawn had gone, there was nothing left to remind her of him except the hole inside where her heart was and the place where he had been for such a short time.

Chapter Forty-Eight
A Wedding

Please join us to celebrate
Our Wedding
Lillian and Barry
Saturday 18th June 1999

<u>**Ceremony**</u>
2 p.m. at Portsmouth Registry office

<u>**Reception**</u>
4 p.m. The Penthouse
Dolphin Court
Southsea

It was such a wonderful occasion to have a wedding for her darling son Barry, and it would mean that all the children would be there to help celebrate with their partners. It was so rare these days to get all of them together in one place as they all had such busy lives.

Gemma had finished at The Priory and had come back to Portsmouth to live and had bought herself a small house. She was attending NA regularly and talked about setting up a business. She had said that she did not want to work at the agency any more but wanted to try something completely different but wanted time to think about what she really wanted to do, perhaps designing clothes for dogs as she had bought herself a dear little shih tzu called Toby and was spending her time trying to find good coats for her tiny dog.

Gemma and Annabel had made peace with each other and were once again close, perhaps they could put behind them the bad times they had gone through soon after the divorce when David had made so much mischief. Gemma had spent time talking to Annabel and telling her why she had spiralled out of control with drugs.

"Mum it all really started with that doctor when he had abused me, I felt so alone and when a friend offered me some coke, I thought that it would take the pain away, and then it just seemed to be a good thing to do whenever I felt depressed. I understand now that it was just a crutch to hang onto and didn't help me at all. But I am in a good place now and I do not need drugs I have so much else in my life."

Simon was bringing his friend Ben as they were a recognised couple now, even David had accepted when he was told that his son was gay and had been very supportive. Annabel had never felt quite so proud of her son Simon when he had told the whole family, it was a very traumatic moment but all they had said was, 'We love you Simon.' The boys were both working in the city and had rented a small flat together, Simon was Barry's best man and was going to spend the night before with Barry as a stag night was planned and he wanted to make sure that Barry was in a fit state the next morning.

Poppy had come down the night before to help Annabel with any last-minute arrangements and her partner was driving down that morning. When Annabel didn't think she could be surprised any more with her children, Poppy had told her that she was pregnant.

"Poppy, that is wonderful news, I couldn't be happier, a grandchild, how lucky I am. have you told anyone else yet?"

"No Mum you are the first person, I don't want to say anything today as this is Barry and Lillian's wedding and I should not take any of the limelight away from them, so please can you keep it to yourself for the moment? Mum we are not planning to get married, we both love each other and don't feel it is necessary to have a piece of paper."

"Darling this is your life and you must do what you feel is right for you, and your baby."

Annabel had offered her apartment for the reception and although the numbers that could be invited would have to be limited it was what the young couple wanted.

The terrace garden looked just amazing with an abundance of flowering shrubs and climbing roses up the wall of the apartment and the storage room in the middle. She had booked a very good caterer who had put up tables on the terrace under sunshades and had dressed each table beautifully. The food would be served from the dining room and the guests could then take their plates either to eat outside or on the tables that had been set up in the lounge. A bar had been set near the front door so when the guests arrived, they could be offered a glass of Champagne, and later help themselves to wine, Champagne or soft drinks.

Gemma and Annabel had gone shopping together in London to buy their outfits and Annabel had chosen a beautiful dress and coat in pale pink with an enormous hat covered in pink roses. Gemma's outfit was much trendier a dark blue trouser suit by Armani with wide, white stripes round the bottom of the fitted jacket, and a white pillar box hat.

Poppy was chief bridesmaid and wore a long dress in beige silk; she looked so beautiful perhaps helped because of the secret she was carrying.

Lilian and her parents were going to meet them at the ceremony, and they were the nicest people offering their help and insisting that they pay for the reception, but Annabel wanted to share the cost which they had agreed to.

David had arrived early accompanied by his latest girlfriend, a young girl that no one had met before and knew nothing about. Annabel thought that it was in bad taste to bring a stranger to his son's wedding, but that was David; he always did what he wanted without any thought for anyone else. The girl was young and was dressed, Annabel thought, most inappropriately in a white dress cut very low so her large breasts were hanging out on show. When they arrived, she asked if she could have a drink and went straight to the bar and proceeded to pour herself a glass of Champagne

At the appointed hour the cars arrived to take the family to the registry office, which was close by and the whole family on arrival took their places. Annabel had arranged for the room they were using in the registry office to be decorated with simple floral displays.

Barry stood at the front of the room with Simon looking very nervous.

There was a hush as the music of *Evergreen* by Barbara Streisand started to play with the arrival of Lillian and her father. She looked stunning in a long, white dress with had an overlay of lace and she was carrying a bouquet of white roses. Poppy and a small child who were the bridesmaids followed.

The ceremony was over when Gemma and Lillian's best friend were called to witness the marriage. It was all over so quickly, and the guests went outside to wait for the bride and groom. A horse and buggy were waiting to take them to the apartment and a great cheer went up as they came out.

The reception was all that Annabel had hoped it would be with the sun shining all day so that the guests could sit outside whilst they were eating and admire the glorious view of the sea, which was a clear blue.

The meal was superb, and much wine was drunk to toast the happy couple.

David was in a great mood going around talking to everyone and spending time with his children which was so nice to see. The only problem was that he didn't seem to be spending much time with his girlfriend who was sitting at a table slowly consuming a bottle of Champagne. Annabel felt sorry for her as she didn't know anyone, so she went over to chat to her.

"Hi, we really didn't get to speak much before, I do hope that you are enjoying yourself."

"It's all right, nice to see how the other half live, I like your flat but it's a little too big for one person. Shame David couldn't live somewhere like this, he told me you took it in your divorce settlement so he really didn't have a choice."

The girl looked at Annabel with envy written all over her face, she picked up her glass and stood up and without saying any more moved over to stand next to David, running her fingers through his hair which he seemed to enjoy.

The day turned into evening and nobody seemed in a hurry to move, so Annabel arranged for the caterers to bring out the small sandwiches and cakes that had been made and she thought that perhaps now was the time to cut the cake.

Barry and Lillian stood next to each other holding the knife while flashbulbs went off for photos,

"Wait a minute," shouted David's girlfriend pushing

everyone out of the way so she could get closer to the table and use her camera. She stumbled as she made her way over and fell onto the cake table which toppled over onto the floor.

There was silence in the room as David and Annabel rushed over, David to help his girlfriend and Annabel to try and rescue the cake. Everyone could see that she was very drunk and great sobs came from her as she stood up and made her way unsteadily to the bathroom.

"Sorry about that, just a little too much Champagne," said David as he hurried after his friend.

Fortunately, the cake was unharmed and was put back onto the table and cut.

The rest of the evening went off without a hitch and Lillian and Barry left soon after to drive to the airport where they were going to catch a plane to Jamaica for their honeymoon. Lillian asked all the single girls to stand behind her as she wanted to throw the bouquet which Poppy caught. She looked at Annabel as she held it in her hands and smiled, perhaps there would be another wedding sometime soon.

David had left soon after the fiasco of the cake half carrying his very drunk friend and without any sort of apology but kissing everyone and thanking them for coming as if had organised and paid for the day.

It was very late that night as Annabel sat on the terrace with a glass of wine. Everyone had left, and the caterers had made a good job of clearing everything away and would come back the next morning to collect the final things.

Annabel had had a wonderful day, but she felt sad that she had no one to share this happy moment with her, she thought back to the special people she had had in her life but felt blessed that she had such wonderful children and friends; perhaps that was all she needed now.

Chapter Forty-Nine
Saving the Best till Last

Annabel had been asked to come to a meeting in London to discuss a proposition for roadshows for regional newspapers. It sounded intriguing as this was what she already was doing for her clients so why they needed to speak with her she wasn't sure.

She arrived at the head office of the newspaper group and was shown into the boardroom and introduced to some of the board members. Coffee was served and she was introduced to all the men in the room, most of whom were the editors of the regional titles. It felt a rather formal meeting just to discuss roadshows, but she took a seat while the chairman started to talk.

"Thank you, Annabel, for taking the time to come and meet with us, we know how busy you are. We have been watching your company for some time now and like what we are seeing, you visit many of the cities where we have a newspaper title and we would like to talk to you about the possibility of asking if you would consider working for us in putting together a roadshow in each of the cities under the banner of the local newspaper. It would enhance the package you are selling to your clients as we would run special advertising prior to the show and then a special pull-out supplement for that week, it would have competitions and special offers for the clients who were featured. We will have built a stage and lighting rig and a video wall where we can run advertisements all day. The rig could then be transported to each city with different branding for that newspaper title. Is this something that might be of interest?"

Annabel took her time to answer as it was a lot to take in and there were some more questions that she needed to ask.

"The stage design and rig, would I have some input into this? And where would it be kept during the months when it was not in use? Also, this would mean a bigger team to sell space, is this something you would agree to."

"You would have complete control of everything and you can choose whoever you wanted to use to build it, and where it would be stored, we are in the business of printing newspapers not organising roadshows so that is why we have asked if you would be interested in running it for us."

"Gentlemen, first I would like to thank you for inviting me here today and I am very flattered to be asked to come and work for this new company, but the question that I must ask is why I need to work for you? It would seem that I would be in competition with myself, as all my time and energies now are focused on promoting my own company and what you are proposing is that I should put that aside and become an employee. So, with many thanks for thinking of me, but I feel that I must decline your offer."

With that Annabel got up to leave, when the chairman asked what a better offer would be.

"I need to think about this, but if you really wanted me to head this up for you, you would need to buy the roadshow diversion of my agency and a really attractive package would need to be discussed."

"Annabel, we thought that we might have to persuade you, so we discussed the following. We will buy the roadshow side of your agency for an amount to be decided, you can still run the agency for the shows, exhibitions and promotions but your clients who now buy into promotions across the country will now be part of this new company. We will pay you a salary fitting with your status as head of this, we will buy you a new car and all expenses for an office staff and warehousing for the roadshow kit. Does that sound like a proposal that would suit you better?"

"Tell me the amount money you are talking for buying me out."

The chairman wrote something on a piece of paper and pushed it across the table to where Annabel was sitting. Annabel looked down and smiled.

"Not quite what I was thinking but I am sure that we can negotiate, but before I agree I must think very carefully if this is the way forward for me. Can you give me a while before I come back to you with an answer?"

"Annabel please take all the time you need, and I am sure that there are more questions that you might need answered, shall we say by the end of the month. We will send you the proposal in writing as you might want to show your solicitor before signing."

Annabel thanked everyone and promised that she would have an answer for them quickly.

What a wonderful offer but was this something she wanted to do? In effect to start again working for someone whom she would have to report to, although the money they were proposing was very attractive her life would not be her own. She needed time to mull over all the pros and cons before she gave them an answer.

It was serval weeks later and she had received the written proposal which she had given to Harry to look through but still had not made a decision. She wanted to clear her head so got the lead for little Toby, Gemma's dog she was looking after for a few days and went out. A walk on the beach was just what she needed.

It was a cold blustery day as she walked along the beach and few people had been brave enough to go out. Toby was playing near the water when she bent down to pick up a shell, when she looked up Toby was nowhere to be seen.

Her heart was beating fast in her chest, oh my God had he gone in the water, she ran down to the sea and could see a little head bobbing up and down, she was near the water when a man waded in scooped the dog up and walked back to her.

"Is this what you were looking for?" he said holding a very wet Toby in his arms

"Oh, thank you, thank you," said Annabel as she took Toby and looked up at the face of the man who had saved him. Time seemed to stand still as she looked into the eyes of Oliver.

"Oliver, is this really you, what are you doing here?"

"Annabel, I have come home, and have come to find you. Your neighbour told me that you had just gone out for a walk and I took a chance that you might be on the beach?"

Annabel did not know what to say, so she just stood there with a very wet dog in her hands when all she wanted was to put her arms round Oliver and hold him close.

"Do you think we might go back to your apartment so that I can dry off and then I can tell you all you want to know, as I am sure that you have many questions."

"I am sorry, you have just saved my dog and all I am doing is standing here staring at you, come on my apartment is just over the road."

Oliver followed Annabel back to her home and she showed him the bathroom, gave him some towels and an old pair of jogging pants that Simon had left.

While she dried Toby off, who didn't seem to be in any distress for having had a swim, she thought of the wonderful thing that had just happened. Oliver was home, but was he staying and did he want to see her, so many questions.

Oliver came into the lounge looking just as gorgeous as when she had last seen him, perhaps a little older, but the crinkles round his eyes suited him and the grey at his temples made him look even more attractive.

"OK Annabel I can see you are just dying to ask me why I am here, so let me help by telling you that I have left the Navy and I returned home about three months ago. My wife and I are divorced, and she has gone back to live with her sister in Cheshire. I wanted to come and find you but I didn't know if that was the right thing to do, I heard that you and David are also divorced but I thought that you might have someone else in your life and didn't want to spoil anything for you. But I just needed to see you again even if you tell me to go away so here, I am."

There was so much that Annabel wanted to say, so much to tell him but to answer his question she moved close to him, put her arms round his neck and kissed him hard.

It was much later when they were laying together on the sofa, and Annabel thought that she had not been so happy as she was at that moment. Thoughts of work did not matter, that could wait until another day all that mattered was that Oliver was here with her.

As music was playing softly, she listened to the words and they seemed to be written just for her: *Save The Best for Last.*

Printed in Great Britain
by Amazon

81683856R00161